Fast Talker

by Michael Mahana

Michaelmahana.writer@gmail.com

For Hermes Peitho, the Persuader

Some people are born salesmen. They start talking and the Charms begin working their magic and you don't even know what hit you as you reach into your pocket and thank *them* when you didn't mean to spend any money at all. You were just looking, just killing time browsing like some grazing animal and suddenly you're dinner on the table for someone living on straight commission.

You have to like a good salesman. They are by nature very likeable. Good salespeople have what the Greeks called *the gift of friendliness,* for they are close to the god Hermes, the handsome god in the running shorts, the one they called *Friend.*

He's the self who never gets stuck in any one place or mood for very long, and his specialty is giving everyone the slip just before the shit hits the fan. That's because friendliness has nothing to do with liking someone. The Customer Service Rep may be friendly and you may even imagine you've made a connection as you chat so amiably, so easily--but the truth is, she's not even there. It's just her Hermes persona flashing the Charms. There's nothing personal about it.

A good salesman makes friends everywhere. He can play you with some subtle or not-so-subtle flattery and attention until you think there's nowhere else he'd rather be than with you and then voila! There's that hand in your pocket again. Someone with the Gift of Friendliness can say or do almost anything and get away with it.

Of course, flattery is easy to recognize for anyone with a shred of Athena's good judgment, but there's always that little Cinderella voice whispering, *the flatterer speaks the truth*, and urging you to believe that you are, indeed, at the center of the world. "Why shouldn't your life be filled with good-looking, friendly people," it says. Close the sale.

Hermes is the light touch that you don't feel until you realize your wallet is gone. That's his brand of intelligence and the reason he's always on the side of survivors.

A good salesman seems to have figured something out about life, some secret you want in on as he shakes your hand with both hands and touches your shoulder so naturally while giving you that big bedroom grin that makes you start to blush. His eyes see right through your thoughts and through your clothes. He's having a great day and so are you.

I met my first salesmen when I was twelve at a cookout my mother threw for the people in the office at Travellers Insurance where she worked as a secretary. All the local sales reps were there, flirting with the secretaries right in front of their husbands, who tolerated it like teenage boys at

Beatles concerts with enough of Athena's common sense to grow their hair long and get out of the way while their girlfriends turned into screaming Maenads, the crazed housewives who followed Dionysus into the hills for his all-night raves.

We were anxiously awaiting the rep from New York City whose name had taken on a mythical dimension through its ritual repetition and praise. Bert Dixon was making a rare appearance in the Providence area that fine summer day. When his green Camaro pulled up the driveway, my pulse quickened along with everyone else's, for I sensed the approach of a god.

His white smile glimmered on his tan face rugged with a two-day beard. He wore dark sunglasses under a baseball cap with a broad brim that made his blue summer suit breezy in the dappled sunlight. I blushed when he kissed my mother's hand.

"My constant life saver," he called her, slipping an envelope into her apron pocket as she thanked him with a sly look. His lapel bore the Travellers' umbrella in glistening diamonds.

Bert's charm infected everyone, drawing them into an ever-widening circle of unabashed admiration. My father's arm went around his shoulder while Mom giggled like a teenager. I had never seen her flirt before.

"Bert, this is our son, Michael," she said, turning the dashing man in my direction.

"Hello, young man," said Prince Charming, as the spotlight lit upon me. "You've got a beautiful mother and a handsome father. No wonder you're so damned good looking."

I curtsied when he offered his large, tan hand and everyone laughed. I was under the spell of a pre-sexual love, the kind that makes boys idolize men they perceive to be good-looking and successful, a survival strategy programmed by the gods.

Bert looked like he lived by a pool with his easy smile of pleasure and getting his way in the world. He stood in the circle telling racy jokes to a crowd under a whammy as he made eye contact with each in turn and threw an occasional glance in my direction. That was when I learned what it meant to have Charisma, another gift of the gods.

Bert only stayed for a hamburger but he was the life of the party. He treated even strangers like old friends and they all went along with it gladly. He raved so much about my mother's green tomato relish that she ran down to the cellar to fetch him the last jar.

When he looked at his watch with dismay, the whole party walked him down the driveway to that green Camaro while he carried a glass of sangria in one hand and jingled the keys like a tambourine in the other. I watched his car disappear around the bend of trees and went back to my room to ponder, awestruck.

I knew Hermes from my book of Greek mythology. I knew that he was my favorite god and the one I wanted most to be like, endowed with the gifts of friendliness, charisma, cosmopolitan charm, and sex appeal. Hermes does things the easy way and he always looks like he's having fun, but beneath the hat and the sunglasses you can never tell what he's thinking.

Stuck in Apollo

The gods choose their friends freely and not the other way around. The thing you love the most may not be where your talents lie, because one god happens to like you and another does not. That can lead to a life that feels like you married the sister of the person you were in love with.

Apollo the Intellectual picked me out at an early age. I'd wake up at dawn and slip downstairs, carefully shifting my weight from step to step to avoid making any noise. My father was a cartographer and his maps enthralled me for hours on end. Rather than playing outside with the neighborhood kids, I memorized coastlines, boundaries, and cities. I rejoiced in discovering curiosities like Llivia in the Pyrenees, Bum Bum on the northeast coast of Borneo, and obscure islands like Bouvet off Antarctica--still owned by the Norwegians. The maps and the encyclopedia were the world I believed in, not the one before my eyes. I was like Persephone in her cave weaving a picture of a world she had never seen.

Apollo sees life as an illusion. He makes you want to rise above mere mortals and dwell in glory among the clouds. He is the voice that says that *in a hundred years none of this will matter and everyone who knew you will be dead and forgotten.* To him, *men's lives are like the leaves of the trees.* We shimmer in the radiance of summer and fall with the brush of the cold, only to be replaced by the new leaves of spring for which we provide the fertilizer. Apollo convinces those who follow him that they are better than ordinary people—until they get old and he pulls the rug out from under them, because even brilliant minds can wind up sitting in a wheelchair hooked up with tubes and staring at the tv screen with no idea who they are. Apollo's a cold one, if unerringly correct.

I walked around school like an alien from another planet. Nothing came naturally. Everyone else seemed to be following some script I never received. I was convinced that the moment I believed in anything, the angels would pull back the curtain and say, "Aha! You've fallen for it. You shall be passed over."

I wrote a poem in the fourth grade:

There is in the back of my mind

That which cannot be governed.

It rules behind, forever back,

Yet won't my eyes let turn.

I wondered how many years God sat there in the darkness before he got around to creating mankind to keep him company. How many candles were on his birthday cake and why couldn't he have done it just one year earlier to soothe his loneliness? God seemed pretty stupid to me.

We went to Montreal for the World's Fair in 1967 where a long rickety wooden bridge terrified the hell out of us and people spoke a language that sounded like ducks quacking. We visited the various national pavilions like walking through the encyclopedia, but what impressed me the most was an exhibition about color blindness at the American pavilion. Everyone kept insisting that the white tubes of light were actually green and that the scrambles of dots had numbers written in them. I didn't see any of it.

I couldn't sleep for a week. I had embarked on the epistemological enquiry of a lifetime. How could I know that what I call *yellow* isn't *blue* to you but you call it yellow because everyone says the sun is yellow and therefore your yellow is a hot color even though it's my blue?

Suddenly it was spring in fourth grade and all the boys knew how to throw a baseball and to jump off the snow drifts on the edge of the parking lot yelling, "Batman!" Somehow they were all grabbing each other's crotches and teasing the girls and the girls were passing notes folded in triangular footballs.

I kept to my books and maps and spent recesses indoors. On lucky days, the teacher let me shake the big brass bell to call everyone back in, which I did with admirable sternness.

In high school, the dentist gave me laughing gas and I had a vision. Under the bright white light in the dentist chair, my body tingled strangely and my brain seemed to split in two: a living body of sensations on the right side and a running commentary on the left trying to keep up as the dentist repeated, "everything's going to be all right." Outside on the sidewalk on that bright day, I saw myself as a complete stranger.

I put aside the maps and turned to the Greek gods to make sense of things. I found a Greek persona for every mood and experience. Once I got the right image, everything took care of itself. What to say and what to do happened as if I was in a state of possession by one or more gods and I didn't have to do anything. I knew I didn't need any additional self beyond the Greek gods, for even the normal self is Athena and the mortal self is Psyche. Nothing is left over.

I was told I had boundary issues. I told my secrets to total strangers and acquired a thick brogue after talking to the exchange student from Ireland for twenty minutes. People looked at me strangely.

By the time I got to Williams College no one could tell if I was brilliant or incredibly oblique. I was dubbed *The Lightbulb* and like Apollo, I was more admired than liked.

My social awkwardness was compounded by my constant crushes on the other male students who were either oblivious or repulsed once they realized what was going on. When I ventured into the gay bars in Boston on summer weekends, Apollo made me long for one man after another until the interest was reciprocated. Once my gaze was returned some glaring fault would present itself, and when I did go home with somcone, all mystery vanished with the orgasm and I knew that this wasn't *the One* I was seeking. Such is the love life of Apollo, who wants you to grasp after things and then turns them into an armful of branches.

Apollo has a low opinion of personal happiness. Rising above life spells out a lonely existence. I learned to scorn business and the love of money, except the inherited money of my lucky classmates whose last names adorned the hills, ponds, and coastal swamps of New England.

Apollo possessed me completely. I wrote poems and burned them on the freshman quad for the gods and only got in trouble for it once. I memorized Plato's *Republic* and took it to heart. I chose to be a *lover of learning*, not a *lover of honor* or *of money,* the bottom rung of Plato's totem pole. *Be true to yourself,* I repeated over and over, *and the rest will follow*--that is, presuming the gods are paying attention.

I was like Psyche walking in adoration among the crowds and then staring at herself in the mirror and feeling only sorrow. I wanted my own Eros, someone better and older than me to yank me up the ladder as the college years flew by like a countdown to Doomsday. When I asked my father for money to travel after graduation, he laughed.

There were no jobs I could think of actually wanting to do except being a professor at college where I could avoid the meaningless life of the great unwashed, so I sent out applications to grad schools.

As I was poring over one of these applications in the cafeteria, a classmate came up to me, looking very serious. It was Steve Case. We could have passed for brothers but that was where the similarity ended. Steve was a man of action, not reflection. He was Another Zeus bound to change the world and reap mighty rewards while I lacked Athena's common sense and questioned the very enterprise of making a living.

"Some of the guys and I are getting computers to talk to each other," he told me, "and I'd like to ask you to join us. I hear you're pretty smart."

"I'm not interested, thanks."

"What is that, German?" he asked, looking at the stack of books on the table. "What are you going to do with German? We're going to make millions."

"I'd rather die than work in computers," I scoffed. He shook his head and walked over to another table.

Steve went on to found America-Online. If I had gone with him, I could have bought my own publishing house and printed my poetry myself. Zeus had offered me a way out of poverty, but Apollo blinded me by telling me to remain true to myself and pursue the study of the gods.

"Your mother and I aren't paying for any more school," my father told me, "especially for a doctorate in Comparative Literature, whatever the hell that is. What are you comparing: different ways to starve to death?"

But the thunderbolt missed and I was whisked from the looming existential *gouffre* by a doctoral fellowship at NYU. For 5 more years, I could immerse myself in the study of archetypes, mythology, and languages, far from Zeus' world of reality. Apollo turned me into a laurel bush at the last minute.

I learned quickly that New York occupies a different psychological terrain than Boston. Apollo owns Boston, where you will be asked where you went to school while you lie on your deathbed, but New York belongs to Hermes where success is all that counts because money is the royal road to pleasure, from art to sex.

I planned on hiding in my intellectual bubble through the dissertation into tenure track and on to retirement without setting foot outside the green quads of academic Arcadia, where my ivory tower would loom over the swarming masses with their sitcoms and their *un-reflected lives which were not worth leading*, as Socrates insisted.

As the train pulled past the horrifying anonymity of Coop City in the Bronx and entered the dark tunnel leading to ugly, promiscuous Penn Station, I entered the heroic night of darkness, immersed in Conrad's destructive element where my soul would be tempered and tested against Joyce's *reality of experience* and Poetry would be forged in the depths of my suffering and study.

At least that was the plan. The very first evening in the City I lost my gold chain to a handsome young man in a dark corner of a bar who kissed me with his hands constantly going up to my neck for the reason I only realized later.

Hermes was ready for me and he didn't let me stay green for long.

His sensibility began to grow on me. I started seeing people differently. So many thousands of faces passing by each day made me see people in types-- social class, ethnicity, and personality types: the expression on one person, the gait of another, the different messages sent by clothing, and the uninhibited interplay of lovers and friends seemed more patterned simply by seeing more of it.

New York has a critical mass of diversity and population that makes the gods more visible. There are business people in suits like herds of Zeus, each one bearing on his face the same worried gravity and mantle of responsibility. There are dignified Athena professionals displaying urbane manners with friends at theaters and restaurants I could never afford. There are homey Hestia's carrying bags of groceries to their coops where they spend the night in with their kitchens and cats. There is Aphrodite galore in the lovers and beauties of both sexes, and all the other gods streaming by in an endless flow that turns individuals into archetypes.

The true inhabitants of the city are the interpersonal selves we share and re-enact over and over again. This is the quality of character that makes New Yorkers so urbane, jaded, and fascinating.

It is a Hermes quality, because Hermes loves a crowd. Crowds are where money is made and love can be found in the most unexpected places. The God of Friends thrives in the ceaseless tide of people whose lives are measurable quantities and to a large degree interchangeable.

And yet he is a loner at heart. Hermes never marries. He is like a traveler whom you can never really know despite his friendliness and even intimacy.

I was no Hermes. I was stuck in Apollo, always lost in thought and trying to rise above things and unable to act spontaneously. All these folks with their careers and relationships were busy little ants while I wandered the sidewalks clutching a book like Ophelia reciting poetry on her way to drowning in ideas and the lack of funds.

Once again, the gods were kind. Eros miraculously came through with a decent place to live on my five hundred dollar a month school stipend. I had been renting a tiny room in Chelsea in an S.R.O hotel from week to week with a shared toilet down the hall and no shower. I bathed with a sponge by the sink and rinsed my hair under the low faucet.

My one luxury was Friday nights at the Duplex, a local piano bar in the Village where unemployed actors got drunk, singing favorites. The waiters knew the clientele was broke and greeted them still in their coats with a demand for an order, so I perfected the art of nursing a single ten dollar cocktail for hours, wetting my lips without drinking and chewing thoughtfully on ice chips in a dry glass. I knew all the tunes and my enthusiasm and youth got plenty of attention.

One night I caught the eye of a man in his forties with a crooked smile and a beard like Poseidon who lived in a fourth floor railroad apartment on Jane Street a short walk away. The room had an alcove with a *la Boheme* view of terraces, a writer's desk fronting a triangle of windows, and the Empire State Building towering in majestic lighting above the rooftops. As Edwin and I dawdled in bed the next morning he told me he was an engineer between jobs and that if I wanted, I could sleep on the day bed in the alcove for three hundred dollars a month.

"Why so little?"

"It's rent control," he said, "I'm not allowed to profit."

Suddenly we were joined by a beautiful silver Persian cat, who landed on the bed with a little chirp.

"Hello."

"That's Dusty," he said. "I found him in the alley in front of the Duplex a year ago. He was a skinny, dirty mess and the friendliest cat I've ever known."

We took a shine to each other immediately. He cuddled gently against my neck and purred.

"I need the extra money while I keep looking for a job," Edwin told me over coffee. "I got an offer—a good offer—in Chicago and I have a connection there---"

I cocked my head. Hermes was holding out.

"Well of course," he admitted. "We fooled around a few times. I'm not keen to leave the City so I took a two-month contract starting in two weeks to see how I like it, and him. You can stay but you have to take care of Dusty. I'll drive back to get him if I decide to stay."

I kept out of Edwin's way as much as I could, getting up before him and packing my things into a neat pile every morning in the corner by the windows. I was as silent as a cat and spent my days studying at the library and at Jean's Patio, a sidewalk café on Greenwich Avenue where the transvestite waiter and the chef screamed at each other in front of the customers and I was told I could occupy a table as long as there were extra tables, "because you're good advertising, honey," the old queen said with an air kiss.

Some god was watching out for me because the job worked out for Edwin and so did the lover. He told me to write three rent checks in a row and when the landlord cashed them I had a right to take over the lease.

"How can I thank you?"

"Keep Dusty and love him," he told me. "My boyfriend's allergic."

My luck was complete. Dusty followed me from room to room and settled down next to me, leaning and purring. He was my precious familiar, my home life, and my awaiting center that I rediscovered whenever I came in from my voyages out in the world--the Hestia to my Hermes.

Even with the low rent it was tight living on my forlorn Fellowship, and that was soon ending. I wore the same tired jeans and t-shirts with dirty sneakers and cut my own hair while prosperity bloomed around me and the building filled up with sharp dressing professionals. They didn't seem so unhappy, despite what Apollo wanted me to believe about working in business.

I spoke to the Department Chair, Anna Balakian, a large, older woman from a family of Armenian refugees who had in the span of a generation assembled a half dozen PhD's at holiday dinners like a gathering of Hyperboreans. She wrote a book on the Symbolist movement decades earlier and had been riding that wave ever since, sending generations of aspiring academics down that particular eddy of poetic history. She sat in the front of the class in a flowing skirt with her legs apart under the desk like the pythoness sitting on her tripod at Delphi, inhaling the fumes. I asked her about the prospect for jobs after the PhD and she looked worried.

"Just don't acquire a taste for money," she warned me in her thick accent, her dark teeth filling me with dread, "or you'll never be a good Comparatist."

But it seemed as though everyone with a trench coat and a briefcase was on to something. I envied the normal folks walking home from their jobs past the doorman, checking their watches, and exchanging pleasantries.

It was the early Eighties and Hermes was in the air. All of a sudden, young people weren't ashamed of loving money. Internships were in and idealism was out. Even our older hippy siblings were starting businesses in high tech and abandoning the candle shops. Now everyone wanted to be Athena the Careerist with her power ties, breakfast meetings, and concern about the direction of interest rates.

"I ought to go down to Wall Street and make a million dollars," I told my father blithely. He loved the idea but cautioned me about the 'million dollars'.

"I am sure it takes one step at a time," he said encouragingly.

Athena and her good judgment were still strangers to me.

Meanwhile, an army of French Apollo's led by Derrida and Foucault were infiltrating Academia and killing all the fun in reading. They disdained loveliness and pounced on any weakness or sentiment with their *signifiers* and *signifieds*. These were the kind of critics who could stand in front of a beautiful painting and talk about the optics, using dense and twisted jargon that won the argument by sheer syllabic intimidation. The rivalry for ever-dwindling tenure track jobs turned those fierce Apollo's into ever-larger fish swallowing each other.

The outlook for the Humanities was grim, never mind for a misfit field like Comparative Literature, the outcast of national literatures. My best hope was for a series of one or two-year adjunct stints far out in the provinces where I'd be forced back into the closet.

Hermes was gaining hold of my soul. I loved the freedom of New York and it took money to live there as anything more than a jealous spectator. Culture and tickets cost a lot. I felt like Hermes when he tells his mother that he isn't going to settle for living in a cave in the boondocks while everyone else is having a rip-roaring time up on Olympus. Besides, I told Apollo, a better profession might give me something to write about besides 'the writing process' that so preoccupied the cynical state-of-affairs dubbed Post-Modernism.

Hermes wanted me to move up to those glamorous coops in the sky. The happy and friendly god has no interest in Apollo's life of privation and scorning the world because the world is where all the fun resides.

I gave a poem to Professor Balakian.

"Offering to Poseidon"

Alone at last in the blue ocean,

Immersed in the cold salty girdle of the Cape,

My arms in the salt-edged wind

That falls summer blue from the gray cliffs at Scusset,

The canal's end, a jettied comma

Letting the Texaco tankers pass

For distant deserts or for Boston,

That city behind the islands.

I stand alone at last

In the cold man of the sand-ribbed sea

Not feeling my feet anymore

As they splash over the gaping clamshells,

The watchful eyes of the man-edged and bucking sea,

The swallower of all things.

My body freezes in the sun-streaked sea

Up to my waist in the freezing August tide

In a place that was once dry land.

The sun looks over my shoulder into the drowned sand,

That infinitesimal mediator of shorelines,

Into its cold white eyes where my toes find their centers.

My eyes catch the white toss of the sun

Off the young waves' frisk,

Their knowing glances that invite me to their cold run.

The sea goes on for miles on three sides of me,

And for once I forget the shoreline

As the salt dries on my cold, wind-licked chest.

She handed me back my poem a week later with an awkward smile, telling me I needed a poetics, a theory to inform my work.

"Take a hint from the Symbolists," she suggested, holding up her book and showing me those dark teeth.

....

"You're a cymbalist?" asked the stranger at the bar, tapping his fingers together. "I used to play the bongos."

I stared past him over the dark heads of the dancing crowd. Then I gave him the obligatory smile, for he had just bought me a drink after watching me stand un-watered against the bar for twenty minutes.

Apollo was getting long in the tooth. All around me there was joking and gossip and the quick replies that leavened city life. I was tired of thinking of twenty dollars as a lot of money.

The next semester I proposed an independent study on the Hermes archetype and got Professor Balakian to agree, relieved to keep me in Apollo mode.

I wanted a new persona. I knew that the ancients used rituals to befriend the gods, and that Step One of any ritual is to get a clear image of the god. This means remembering his aspects—the good and the bad--because half of loving someone is just knowing him and the other half is sticking around despite what you find out.

I needed a clear image of Hermes. The literature and imagery are vast, and he is far more than a simple Trickster. Hermes is the elegant cosmopolitan, the tour guide, the clever word, the persuader and seducer, and the person with news and ingenuity. One touch of his staff on the forehead bewitches you, sends you to sleep, or keeps you from noticing what's going on right before your eyes.

The God of Twists and Turns likes boxing, running, wrestling, and all manner of competition. Those twists and turns extend into hermeneutics, the art of interpretation, which changes reality by seeing it differently. He is the magician, the deceiver, and the liar. He is the elegant gentleman and the roughhouse thief like his son, Autolyus. His intelligence is not Apollo's intellect. Hermes is clever, not brilliant. His smarts are street smarts and invention, like short cuts, clever ideas, and dusting off old ideas and putting them back into circulation.

The God of Travelers takes you across the psyche, visiting one mood and then the next. To him, experience is an archipelago of selves, and no person or situation is completely devoid of virtues because *this too shall pass*. Even a Cyclops is good for a few laughs because soon enough you'll be talking to someone else.

Apollo can keep his love of idealized Beauty, Art, and Truth. When Hermes leads the Muses, it's a best seller or a solid gold record. His refinement is not truth, purity, or understanding, but artifice, pleasure, and cultivation. A good salesman or servant isn't *being himself* just because he seems relaxed while performing his artifice. Hermes knows how to smile when needed, not only when it's real.

I tried to notice him in everyday situations: in people, places, things, and events that matched his personality and style. I saw him in the friendly gesture, in the ambiguous wave of the hand, in the smile of the stranger or acquaintance that reveals some things while concealing others. I saw him in the bar, looking around and assessing, and at the gym, chatting someone up.

He is the mood that pops up out of nowhere like a stranger asking for directions. His *hermaion* is the lucky find, the letter with good news, and the chance encounter that starts with a glance over a drink or on the sidewalk. I started seeing Hermes everywhere. He's anyone or anything that's on its way somewhere else.

Some people seem to embody him, but most people reflect him only in passing moments: the dull librarian grins slyly; the banker flirts; and the man in the wheelchair shares a private joke with his nurse. The gods can take any shape that can be personified and they dwell in the meaning of the experience, so they're never hard to find.

As I studied his stories and statues, I tried to think of Hermes as a person and not only as a concept. If the gods are the people dwelling within, they surely don't want to be thought of only intellectually, as Apollo would have you do.

Step Two of any ritual is to establish a rapport with the god, because asking for the gifts of a god without putting a friendship in place is like walking up to a stranger and asking for a loan.

I knew it was easier to recognize an existing friendship than to start one from scratch so I started scouring my memory for instances of Hermes trying to break through.

First off, I was always a smart aleck. I was voted Class Chatterbox in high school and our yearbook shows me begging my female counterpart for the telephone in the bushes out by the school parking lot. My expertise was in running a commentary during class up to the exact point when the teacher gets truly annoyed, and then sitting back wearing an angel face while some Herakles pushes him one step too far and bears his pent-up wrath. I called that 'stepping out of Zeus' way' and it was pure Hermes, who knows how to avoid conflict.

Having to conceal my gayness in a Catholic, military family had honed my skills at deception, another Hermes aspect. My father would never have paid for my expensive education if he thought he was sending his gay son to finishing school. Sneaking around for sex is a kind of thievery, because Hermes doesn't have to own things or marry them to enjoy them.

But the thing at which I exceled as Hermes was in my love and gift for languages. I marveled at the Polish countess in "Death in Venice" who spoke to everyone in his native language, switching easily from French to German to English to Polish. She seemed so mysterious; who was she behind all those languages? The countess became the Queen of my psyche, my Heavenly Aphrodite, and I was enthralled by anyone who could move among languages like the God of Tongues.

I had spent sophomore year in France. I saw the other American students hanging out together, thrilled to discover how cool it was to be American, and never learning much French. I didn't want to be an American speaking French, I wanted to be a Frenchman, so I invented a French self, sketched out a bit of personal history—I was from Bordeaux, married with children, and imagined a scene in a field by a fence—and let that person do the talking.

My French took off. My French friends couldn't believe what they were hearing. The greatest thrill was having trouble getting back into English in the car from the airport. Hermes was thrilled.

I took Beaudelaire's speculation that '*je* est un autre'—*I* am an Other—one step farther: *je* sont des autres—I am Others. There is no self to hold onto, only selves. Even the Real Self is just Apollo, and it's just one self among others, the one who provides the feeling of being real.

I kept this way of looking at things to myself because I knew people would think I was crazy, but since the gods don't like secrets I spoke of nothing else, and my obsession with the Greek gods became a running joke with my friends and our shared private language.

"What god is it when I want to scream in the middle of a crowd?" asked one.

"Pan," I said without losing a beat. "He is panic and the Self Who Runs Amok."

"What god picks his nose?" asked another.

"Some sea creature of Poseidon, I suppose," I said, "since that shows a lack of sociality and complete immersion in sensation."

Other Hermes qualities came to light. Sometimes I enjoyed shocking people, and I was always more interested in ideas than in people.

Apollo admires his little brother, but he doesn't always approve of him, like the time he caught him rustling his cattle and hauled him up to Zeus. Hermes was only a baby then but he picked Apollo's pocket and then pooped in the arms of his accuser. Apollo is just as shocked as the ladies when Ares is caught naked with Aphrodite under Hephaestus' net, but Hermes gladly offers to switch places, even with all the goddesses looking on in disapproval—a compliment that Aphrodite does not fail to reward. Now Hermes calls whenever he's in town and they share an evening of delight, using each other freely.

He is the pillar of stone found at the crossroads and boundaries all over Greece carved with only a smile and an erection, said to be gazing upon the naked Persephone or Artemis. A lot of cruising went on in those old crossroads. Traveling makes people horny because Hermes is always on the lookout for sexual opportunity and is a founding member of the mile-high club.

I *gave* him my experiences in the infamous seventh floor bathroom in the Main Building at NYU where there was a glory hole between the stalls. He was the thrill at the possibility of being caught under the net by my professors and colleagues. He was the flushed face I wore to my seat in class looking as if I had just come in from running or dancing like Paris, fresh from love-making with Helen. It wasn't *I* who

35

acted; it was Hermes acting through me. He loves the danger of discovery and disapproval.

He is the comic erection of the honeymoon, when the guy pulls his pockets out and zips his fly around his penis, trumpeting a Bronx cheer and calling himself an elephant. He is the shock of the erection in the most inappropriate situations, and its comedy.

He is the one who slips in after a night of sexual escapades without a sound. Cavafy writes about the god sneaking down from Olympus at night to seek pleasure among mortal men, and not *The One True Love* of Apollo.

I *gave* those nighttime adventures to Hermes by seeing him acting through me, and as my repertoire with the god increased, the friendship grew stronger. I saw his Underworld aspect in the strange feeling of leaving a movie theater in mid-day and discovering that it's still light outside as the stories and characters from moments ago dissolve like dreams and life resumes its normal Athenian reality. I admired how professionals in any line of work can set aside their personal selves as easily as picking up the phone and suddenly there is another voice that speaks, an altered posture, and a different person altogether.

This ability to see yourself as someone else seemed to be the key to happiness, because if you can fit your persona to the setting, you can get along anywhere.

Step Three of any ritual is the exchange of gifts. A ritual gift can be anything at all so long as you perform the action as if you are the god and not just as yourself. By assuming the very virtues you seek, the god infuses you with his gifts, and eventually the persona takes on a life of its own like a kind of muscle memory for the brain.

The only requirement for a gift to a god is sincerity. Who wouldn't be honored by someone dancing around the room waving an ostrich feather and singing his praises on his birthday? The gods love unusual gifts, and the price of the gift matters little to them, for they are rich already. What they really want is to share in our experience and for us to invite them to live through us.

In the statuary Hermes is often shown running. I was never a gifted runner but I found that if I pretended I was carrying a message it gave me a sense of urgency and suddenly it was as though a stranger was running through me, dodging people on the sidewalk like a man possessed.

As I leaned on the bannister of the stairs leading up to my apartment, dripping in my running shorts, I would announce, "That was Hermes running, not me."

Luckily I was alone.

In the apartment, I daubed my wet fingers in the ashtray and drew warrior lines across my cheeks to estrange my face. Standing in front of the bathroom mirror, I turned out the lights and closed the door, staring nose to nose with my reflection. My face began to morph within moments.

"I am Hermes," I told the mirror, and the eyes looked back at me from their dark space with a strange intelligence. It was difficult to keep looking. Suddenly I was an old man, then a shriveled peasant woman, then a sad boy. I performed this little ritual every day after the main run and before jumping in the shower, dedicating the whole ceremony to Hermes.

My body changed rapidly. In a month my body cut up and my face looked gaunt.

"Are you eating enough?" asked Professor Balakian, looking worried. "How's your health?"

We had never discussed my gayness but the Department had already lost one scholar to AIDS.

"I think I'm growing taller," I improvised and she gave me a curious look. That was a Hermes evasion, so I dedicated it to the god. I avoided her eyes and stared at her dark teeth, concealing my horror in an exaggerated smile.

The final break with Apollo came at the grocery store when I was caught short at the register and had to put back the ground beef for the spaghetti I was making that night. Someone sighed behind me in line and I blushed under the scornful eyes of half a dozen busy people.

I was done sacrificing to Mr. Nothing in Excess. The Doomed Poet act wasn't working for me if I couldn't even make a meat sauce at home.

At the beginning of the Homeric hymn, Hermes walks out of his mother's cave looking for some meat to eat. He is healthy greed, the normal human desire to get a piece of the pie and a bite of the apple. Meat was wealth in the old days and here I was eating plain pasta with butter and pepper for dinner and tomato sandwiches for lunch.

"I'm taking a semester off," I informed Professor Balakian. She sat up in alarm, her teeth darkening out a frown.

"Is it money or is it your health?"

"I'm not finished with Hermes," I answered, holding up my notebook. "I've got to do some personal research on the subject."

I left her office before she could answer, but when I turned around she was holding up her book and shaking her head.

I disappeared like a stranger at a bar who says he's going to the bathroom and will be right back. Over the years, I wanted to call Professor Balakian and I was sad to read of her death in the newspaper, but she was my first sacrificial victim to the new god I chose to serve.

I wanted to eat meat. It was time to *live like a bourgeois and think like a demi-god* as Flaubert advised, and to stop feeling noble and resentful as both Psyche and Stomach cried out for attention.

I met my first banker at Julius, the oldest gay bar in the Village. Jim was a slim man with the thin, nasal accent of Chicago. His sharp mind was given to compulsive punning and double entendres. He was a preppy variation of Hermes with a mania for success in business. He quickly figured out that I was a starving grad student and spared me the embarrassing questions. He was subletting an adorable hidden cottage in a courtyard near Washington Square for the summer.

"This must cost a fortune," I said, admiring the hidden patio.

"I rented it fortune-to-September," he said. I looked at him quizzically.

"I'm gonna call you Banana," he announced, handing me a scotch and soda.

"Rhymes with Mahana," I said, remembering high school.

"This is the summer of no masturbation," he announced as he proudly unbuttoned his jeans. "Summer bigger than others."

His large penis hung magnificently against his slim body like another Priapus, the little garden god who trips over his hoe-size member.

We lay musing on the bed after sex.

"So you want to make a million dollars by the time you're thirty," I repeated.

"No, Banana, I want to make a million dollars a year by the time I'm thirty. Anyone can make a million dollars by thirty."

He was a mover and shaker out to conquer the world. He spent every waking minute packaging real estate partnerships, even working Sunday mornings. I admired his self-discipline and wondered that anyone could be so passionate about limited partnerships.

"Do you need an M.B.A. to work downtown?" I asked, hopelessly naive.

"No, Banana, not if you just want to be a stockbroker. All you need for that is to know how to hustle."

"How much do they make?"

"The sky's the limit. It depends on how much you work and how smart you work. You have to like cold-calling."

"Calling a stranger from a list?"

"That's all it takes, Banana," he said, relishing my new nickname. "The ability and willingness to cold call. Nothing else matters. It's a numbers game, pure and simple: call enough people with a stock and eventually someone will buy it. Do that enough and you've got a list and you're working for yourself. Sometimes I wonder why I spent so much time and money at grad school when I could've just been a stockbroker."

After a couple of tricks we settled into a typical gay friendship, calling each other up to go cruising in the Village and in the emerging scene in Chelsea. Watching how easily he reached into his pocket sparked a desire for money that I saw as a healthy dose of Hermes, the God of Profit. I kept peppering Jim about how to become a stockbroker. Always he came back to cold calling, the horrible truth about sales and the thing everyone hates about salesmen.

"Not if you're good at it," he assured me. "Good salespeople make it look easy—and they enjoy going in for the kill."

When Jim took a job offer in San Francisco, we met at the bar for a parting drink. There was no pretense at keeping in touch. Ours was a provisional friendship—a Hermes style friendship. I didn't expect to see him again, but he said that if he ever moved back to the City he'd get back in touch.

"Hasta manana, Mahana Banana," he said, pronouncing it *Ma-hah-na, Ba-nah-na* for the sake of the rhyme.

"Hasta la pasta," I quipped.

That's how Hermes is with his friends. When he's in town, he gives you a call and everyone has a good time. There are no demands but there is good will and loyalty tempered by realism. That's how his affair went with Aphrodite, and it was the longest lasting affair on Olympus.

"Let's just always bring the best to each other," he said as the ice cubes clicked in our drinks.

I called the Office of Career Counseling at Williams. They gave me a name from the Class of '28, Benjamin Coffin, from an old family on Nantucket.

"A stockbroker!" My father was beside himself with glee. "I'll buy you a blue suit so you'll look sharp for interviews."

We went to Sears where he bought be an eighty-dollar suit made of Super Silk, a weave of polyester that glistened in the sunlight.

I headed downtown a couple of hours before the interview to get a feeling for Wall Street, keeping to the shady side of the street to avoid shining in my suit. The crowd was in a perpetual hurry. It was thrilling.

There were mostly men in suits but there was also a tribe of blue-suited Zeus-type women in skirts. Most of the female sex, however, were on the young side with fussed up hair and make-up out of "Guys and Dolls".

I exulted at the prospect of working with so many smart and good-looking people and marveled at how Money attracts the Beautiful wherever it accumulates.

I also saw the toll that Wall Street takes. The older men were fat from inaction or strangely deformed by their jobs. Some walked with a hunch to the right as if the telephone was always pinched between their ears and shoulders. Others loped along with one arm swinging like a single celled creature. Still others hunched their shoulders from saying, 'I don't know' for so many decades.

Theirs was a Faustian bargain, trading youth and vitality for money and guarantees. With all the naivete of youth, I swore never to let work keep me from staying in shape, no matter how demanding the job. That was a vow to Ares, who is Virility.

The Exchange tour lasted an hour. After viewing a few antique tickers I entered the great room of the New York Stock Exchange.

The air was as crisp as fresh dollar bills. Outside the walls of bulletproof glass the room roared like a giant beast as a riot of men shouted at each other and gesticulated wildly—

and the newspapers said the next day that the markets were sluggish. I bathed in the electric aura of wealth and deal-making below the glassed-in bridge over the great Chamber of Capitalism, a Temple of Hermes where fortunes are made and lost as the electronic ticker flows along the walls like a river in the Underworld, spelling out doom and destiny. Here Fortune works recklessly across the vying souls, tearing this one apart, endowing that one with undue riches, making and ruining individuals, dynasties, corporations, and nations in the constant and urgent flow of the mercurial cosmos. Men crowded together on the floor below me staring at charts and divining Fortune's next move like priests of Hermes gazing at the night sky and calculating the trajectories of stars and planets.

My eyes settled on one man by the GE desk, a handsome man in his forties, dark and trim in tight black slacks. He wore the requisite blue jacket of the Market Maker and was given to elbowing his comrades with a wise crack smile.

None of his moves seemed extraneous. He wasn't showing off. The crowd was his element. They knew him and liked him. At one point, his dark eyes wandered up in my direction and I caught his glance, but he looked down again and did not repeat the gesture.

I carried that image of Hermes with delight as I walked up Wall to Trinity Church and settled in a pew to gather my thoughts. John the Baptist looked down at me from the stained glass window with the fire around his feet. I thought about the man on the floor of the Exchange and prayed to Hermes for good luck.

Jim and the author in the early '80s

The Friendly God

The lobby of the slick blue-glass building at Thirty-three Whitehall Street is black granite with a low, polygon-shaped black pool dribbling over into a tiny moat. The motif of the building is a black granite needle resting on a tripod of black granite balls, one at each corner of the lobby. Freud would have loved the place.

The elevator opened into a wood-paneled hall where the receptionist told me to sit by a door that led directly into Coffin's office. Opposite me was a glass door peering over the Harbor, promising a tremendous view from the glass walls within. I sat nervously fidgeting with my fingers and trying to think about Hermes. Finally the receptionist told me to go in.

"So you're interested in retail?" asked Gerald Coffin, Class of '28, getting up from his desk. He looked like Ichabod Crane and reeked of old money and oldness in general as he reached a craggy hand in my direction, surprising me with his vigorous grasp, like a dying man making one last point.

"Yes," I answered, unsure. This wasn't a retail store; it was an office, but I played along, staring at his desk and trying to relax.

Father Zeus was not deceived.

"There's retail and there's institutional," he clarified, "and you'd already know if you were going to the institutional side. Either you're a stockbroker for individuals which is retail or you work for some large fund or institution--a family trust, for instance."

He leaned forward inquisitively and my blank stare told him I was not one of the rich kids from Williams sent to manage the family fortune. I was one of the financial aid students scooping ice cream for them in the cafeteria.

He must have been eighty years old in his musty pinstripe and yet his eyes were lively and scrutinizing. Here was Cronus, the King of the Golden Age who rules Elysium's hidden paradise in the remotest reaches of the Underworld, looking me up and down and weighing my soul. I began to sweat in my shiny suit.

"Let's talk about retail," he relented. "Come look at the Boardroom."

I was ushered into a vast office with three continuous walls of glass open to the surrounding skyscrapers and New York Harbor. From this high vantage, Governor's Island floated below like a ship and the Statue of Liberty loomed close in the harbor like Athena, guarding her fair city. The water seemed to have been cut by a palette knife with scalloped white edges scudding across the plane of blue green.

The room was busy with men talking into headsets and peering anxiously into screens while the electronic tape raced along the top edge of the walls with its continuous stream of coded information as though the very room were thinking. The old man's eyes kept drifting up to the stream of numbers and symbols with its hypnotic power and made a hundred little reactions to the prices racing by as we drifted around the buzzing office.

I felt woefully unprepared to compete in this sophisticated and dynamic financial society where world events alter the course of the day and instantaneous decisions are constantly being made. The glacial pace of academic life looked parochial next to the volcanic, tectonic momentum enlivening these men. The ticker rushed by like a waterfall as dozens of conversations were spoken at once, jokes told, and deals closed. I was surrounded by a lingo I didn't understand, but it was clear that everyone was telling someone else what to do: exhorting, convincing, or pleading over the phone. I was adrift in a sea of Hermes' words of persuasion—speech with a purpose--and marveled at the decisiveness that animated the crowd.

"It's very exciting," I told my ancient guide, frantic to cover my stage fright. I knew I had to say something but Virgil nodded absently and kept his eye on the tape that slipped by like the ever-rushing Present.

"So how long have you been downtown?" I asked, trying to keep him engaged.

"Been here since forty-four," he answered without moving his eyes from the tape. "I started running tickets for traders and rose on my own talent. After thirty years, I tried to retire. I'd made my money and thought I should get out and enjoy the fruits of my labor, have a Tom Collins by the pool, maybe do some fishing. But I was dead wrong. I couldn't keep my nose out of the paper."

I knew he meant the Wall Street Journal and not the New York Times.

"By the time we were alone together for six months, my wife told me either I had to go back to work or she'd start drinking before noon."

A roguish grin lit up the ruins of his old face and for a moment I could see that he was once a handsome young man and that was he still in love with his wife. He was not just an old Cronus. Hermes was still with him, and I recalled several vases with an elderly variation of Hermes.

It never occurred to me that anyone would spend an entire lifetime on Wall Street. I thought Wall Street was like the California Gold Rush: you make some dough and get the hell out--maybe open a gym, a restaurant, or a bed and breakfast. How interesting could it still be after all those years? What use was the money if it only made you want more?

This was my first encounter with the common foot soldier of Wall Street, the Workaholic. It turns out that people who live on commission never take vacation and never retire. When they get old they just show up market hours and stop taking on new clients. The Market is a Hermes addiction and it holds people as surely as the Sun holds the planets in orbit. Everyone's afraid of missing out on something so they stay on like surfers at sundown trying to catch one last wave. It's the gods they're after, not just the cash.

I was surrounded by the thrill of the hunt as the electronically charged words darted about like a rain of arrows. The psyche down here was more complex than I had anticipated with my Apollo bias against people who actually work for a living.

"When I came back, they put me in charge of the Boardroom to instill some values and work ethics into this Ivy League flotsam," he said rather loudly, "Mostly hustlers and thieves, not that they aren't some great fellows too. We've had hot ones here, guys you couldn't hold down who soared and made money right out of the gate. But we easily get a hundred times as many who flash in the pan and fizzle out—or get scorched with a reneg. Now they're doing something else for a living, or they're in rehab."

He laughed and gave me a searing look. I tried to appear as sober as possible.

"I still manage my own accounts. Everyone in management has to keep his hand in the business. We don't want a bunch of theorists running the sales department. God no! But mostly, I just try to keep the Boardroom clean as a whistle and stave off the lawyers and settlements…"

His voice trailed off as his eyes caught something on the omnipresent tape, racing by like a river of money. The late afternoon sun came sidelong through the windows as the men continued this rarefied Stone Age hunt with shirtsleeves rolled up and ties loosened, their faces tense with meaning amid the constant ringing of telephones like the strange calls of the lush, prehistoric forest. They were hunting alone and in teams, scouting for food and mates and luxury apartments, armed only with the telephone, a list of prospects, and quick wits. How nerve wracking it all seemed. What a thrill it must be when you cover your bills every month and the rest is profit. And how exciting to be able to make more money simply by working harder and staying late or coming across a winning streak.

He pointed out two slim, Mediterranean looking fellows in their early thirties. One was leaning back from his desk with one hand supporting the phone on his shoulder, talking softly--whether to a customer or to a lover, it was impossible to tell. The other was staring at the screen and listening to someone on his headset as he wrote out a ticket. In their tailored suits they were prime catches for husband hunters.

"Those two have what it takes," he said loudly enough for the ones around them to cringe in their seats. "They've got the right attitude and they know how to move money in and out of situations. Most of all they know how to open accounts, unlike the rest of this gang of bozos."

His face was cold and terrible. I shrank before this other Cronus, the one who ate his children.

"We ought to fire the whole bunch and start over again," he announced to the room at large, looking as though he was about to do just that, "and get some motivated salespeople in here for a change."

The brokers working around us registered his proclamation with a slight, nervous shifting of position in their chairs. They were on the phone in an instant.

"We don't sell lumber here," he informed me, "We sell ideas. What is a bond or a stock certificate beyond the nifty graphic and the paper it's printed on? All that counts down here is the ability to sell ideas and dreams to a total stranger and get him to send you a check. You need enthusiasm, good habits, and the ability to tell a story. That's what you're here to do, not spend the day looking for dividends, calling your girlfriend, or chatting up the poor. Market hours are for finding new pools of money. New accounts are the lifeblood of this business."

We were standing in front of the door to his office. A harried older secretary with a round Irish face barked at him, "Ben, you have Legal on one, Josephine from Corporates on two, and Nick on three. Margin has two sell outs in half an hour with a ten thousand dollar reneg to the broker."

This was the tough older version of the Mexican sunset girls I saw on the street, rolling her eyes impatiently as she wedged herself between us. My job connection was about to give me the slip.

"You never know who's going to be on the other end of the phone," he told me, summarizing quickly. "That next call could be your biggest client, or it could be his best friend, or his accountant--you just never know. It's a numbers game. If you make a hundred phone calls a day—and I mean a hundred connections, not a hundred dials—you'll open one account a day. Open ten accounts and you'll open one decent account. And if you can get a hundred of those together you'll have a business."

"Ben," the secretary growled, flashing a Medusa face at me.

"Gotta go," he said, shaking my hand. "Remember, if you build a business down here and treat it right, it's an annuity for life. Many thanks. Let us know where you end up."

"What should I do next?" I asked in a panic.

"How should I know?" he said as closed the door.

Out in the lobby by the elevators, I wondered what happened. The interview had gone so well and then suddenly it was over. No mention of a second interview or a job. As the elevator dropped me back down from Olympus my mood fell along with it. At home, I threw myself on the bed, bewildered.

I was afraid of Wall Street. How was I going to become one of those dynamic young men when I was a self-conscious Apollo: intellectual, hesitant, and painfully awkward? Friendliness did not come naturally to me.

Clearly I needed to intensify my rituals if I was going to get past the interview. I improvised an altar by putting tea candles in the non-working fireplace and rummaging around for whatever knickknacks and items I could think of to evoke the god.

There was the silver dollar my grandfather gave me, a ceramic Peter Pan figurine from Disneyworld, and a AAA pen-flashlight as a symbol of Hermes the Traveller. To symbolize Hermes' roving sexuality, I placed a metal cock ring in front of Peter Pan and resolved to wear it whenever I needed his good luck.

I re-read his myth in my worn copies of Robert Graves and H.J. Rose and tried to imagine what it's like to be Hermes.

Then I burned a stick of Jasmine incense I bought from the Senegalese hawkers on Sixth Avenue in a glass on the tiled hearth. On the mantle I arranged some green apples from the corner fruit stand and a postcard of Hermes by Praxiteles I had found at the Met.

I donned my running shorts, a t-shirt, and sneakers as a kind of vestment ceremony, thinking of Hermes while I did it. The room smelled of balsam as I stood before the little altar with arms out in ritual greeting pronouncing, "Hermes".

I imagined the god as an invisible presence in the room.

"Hermes, you are likeable, you are clever. You are the god who loves changes and quick turns. I've always admired you. You are one of the most beautiful Greek gods, and those who call you 'friend' are among the luckiest people on Earth."

I figured that should take care of Step One: remembering the god. Now for Step Two: establishing a connection.

"I've always loved languages and traveling like you," I continued. "I was good at making wise cracks and getting away with it. I love sex for pleasure and for its own sake. And I love to run."

That was all I could think of for the moment to qualify myself as a friend of the god, someone he should bother doing favors for.

"Those moments were you acting through me," I added, sweeping my hands as though giving those memories to the god.

Now for Step Three: the request.

"Make me your friend and mold me in your likeness."

I tried to imagine the essence of the god filling me from the feet up like water pouring into an empty vessel. I imagined my mortal self as Psyche taking one step to the side as the god filled me and possessed my body. Then I took one of the green apples from off the makeshift altar and held it up to the image.

"Consider this apple a gift to you," I said, "I hope you enjoy the taste."

I ate the apple standing in front of the altar and tried to imagine swallowing the god's essence, like at Communion.

"Now," I told Peter Pan, "I am going to give you three more gifts."

I slipped on the cock ring from the altar, nodded at Peter Pan and walked out to the street, pretending to be Hermes. First I greeted a total stranger on the sidewalk with a vigorous 'hello' and kept on walking. Then I saw a tourist puzzling over an unfolded map and offered him directions, which he gladly took. As I went back into my building I saw the woman who lived next door with whom I had previously shared only polite nods and asked her as she stood holding a couple of bags of groceries, "What's the difference between roast beef and pea soup?"

"I don't know. What?" she said, startled and pleased at my unaccustomed friendliness.

"Anyone can roast beef," I answered, giving just the right pause between *roast* and *beef.* A moment later, she laughed. We finally introduced ourselves and promised to exchange keys in case we ever got locked out.

"I'm taking a nap now," I said, handing her back her bags, both of us smiling.

When I awoke two hours later my eyes fell upon a ceramic duck I had bought a couple of years earlier at Macy's, something I had never meant to buy and certainly couldn't afford but somehow was talking into buying and there it was, gracing the shelf in the bedroom.

The woman who sold it to me was an older Jewish lady in a pink pantsuit with several strings of beads dangling between her small breasts. Her wrists jingled with bracelets and she wore giant gold hoop earrings and enormous T.V. screen sunglasses to ward off the bright lights of the store. She stood with a slim, straight elegance and looked every bit the Long Island suburban grandmother.

She watched me peering at the duck from the counter and as I started to walk away, she swooped to my side like a bird alighting on a branch.

"It's a nice one, isn't it?" she asked, picking it up and admiring it.

"Yes," I answered, "I've always liked decoys."

"It's top quality," she assured me, placing it in my hands.

I agreed and started to hand it back to her but she stopped me.

"Shall I wrap it or is it a gift to your self?" she asked.

"Oh no," I said, alarmed. "I was just looking."

"You've been *just looking* for twenty minutes," she said with amusement. "You want this duck. I see it in your face. And it's a beautiful duck, and I believe it's the last one in stock. It's from Maine--see? It's signed on the bottom."

She turned it upside down in my hands to show me the signature of someone named Peithos.

"I don't want it," I insisted, "I'm a starving student."

"I knew you had a studious look," she observed. "I can smell intellect a mile away. What do you study?"

"Comparative Literature, Doctoral program," I gave the well-practiced reply.

"So you're some kind of genius. How could you not want this duck? It's so preppy it's perfect for you. What, don't you like it?"

"That's not the question."

"I bet you could use something elegant and traditional like this on your desk, couldn't you?"

"Yes."

"Haven't you read enough literature to know that this has totemic value?" she asked, jolting me with the phrase. "This could be a good omen for you. Ducks symbolize wealth, especially old money."

I held the porcelain statuette as she kept smiling and looking at me.

"And it's only thirty dollars," she continued, suddenly looking concerned. "I can't believe that's the right price. I ought to check that, I thought they were sixty. Perhaps it's mislabeled. Just a moment please," she said, "Don't go away, I'll be right back."

She disappeared behind a door to the back room while I stood holding the duck for a few moments. I considered putting it down and fleeing but she was back in an instant with a puzzled look on her face.

"The manager is out and that's the last one so there's no one around to confirm the price so it has to go for thirty dollars," she sighed. "I don't know how that sticker got on it but our strict policy is to sell as advertised even if it's a mistake which this definitely seems to be. Do you have a special affinity for ducks?" she asked, looking up brightly.

"I had a duck pond growing up in Rhode Island," I told her proudly.

"How lucky," she exclaimed, "To grow up in the country."

A girl from Long Island should be no stranger to ducks, but I said nothing as she took it from my hands and carefully placed it in a green box that she produced from under the counter. Then she removed the price tag, shaking her head as if in resignation and wrapping the duck in green tissue and tying the box with gold ribbon. She handed me the box and took my credit card with an approving smile.

"We had twenty three ducks at one time," I volunteered nervously, "All from two original ducks."

"Well," she laughed, "I guess that's how it works."

Her laughter shook her baubles and small breasts like a shaman doing a medicine dance as she slid the card through the machine. Her good mood was contagious.

"So did you ever try the eggs?" she asked, handing me a pen and the slip to sign.

"I fried one once but it smelled too strong and the size was creepy."

"Gamey, too, I'm sure. This fellow's a classic. Were your ducks white or were they mallards like this one?"

"They were white."

"Well this is the kind of duck you'll find out in the wild. The male is more beautiful than the female," she added, giving me an inquisitive look as she handed me back my card with the receipt. "You've made an excellent purchase."

As the image of that charming and persuasive lady floated back to me, I realized she was a female Hermes, the first of three women who were to teach me about this god like the Three Graie, the ancient goddesses who lived in a cave and shared a tooth, an eye, and a hoop earring among them.

And then it dawned on me why the old man hadn't offered me a job.

I hadn't asked for it.

The gods send blindness to hide what they are doing. The Greeks considered *Ate,* or Blindness, to be a person in her own right, imagined as a cloud hovering around the shoulders. I was exasperated at my stupidity.

If internships on Wall Street are a one-way ticket to orchestra seats and expensive suits in the big city, then I had failed the most basic test of Hermes: I hadn't asked for the order. I was waiting for the job to be conferred upon me like Apollo's laurels.

I knew there was no changing one's own nature. I was a friend of Apollo and the gods cannot be shoved aside, but they don't mind if you make friends with other gods. Apollo would not begrudge my befriending Hermes so long as I remembered him and kept at my poetry. In that moment the decoy duck became Apollo and the life he had given me, so I placed it to the side of the hearth of my makeshift altar out of the way of the other images.

"You belong here, too," I reassured the little statue. "I promise that one day I will return and give you my complete attention once again."

I called Coffin's office back but he didn't return my call, so I feared my one chance with him was spent.

But that night, I woke up thinking about the Long Island saleslady again. She hadn't given up when I refused. She kept trying different angles and going for the close until I relented.

Suddenly the rituals took on urgency. My back was against the wall and the future was no longer just an intellectual exercise. The fellowship was ending next semester and I would have no income at all. So I obsessively followed the three traditional steps of any ritual: getting a clear image of the god, pointing out my past friendship with him, then asking for his gift while performing an action in his likeness.

The display at the altar kept growing: a rabbit's foot, a pair of dice, a deck of cards--until there was quite a collection of honorifics around the white painted brick fireplace.

I tried to visualize Hermes pouring into my body through any metaphor I could think of: a glass filling with liquid, a statue being covered in gold, a picture coming into focus. Always I would say some variant of, "Hermes, fill me with your persona, take possession of me."

After performing my three daily gifts, I would stand again in front of the altar and say, "Thank you, Hermes. That was you acting and not me."

The gods are like people. Their friendship cannot be forced. I continued the daily rituals for a week after my inauspicious interview. When I called back Ichabod's office his secretary informed me sternly that he was busy so I slipped on my lucky Hermes cock ring and showed up in my shiny pinstripe suit again and told her I would wait in the reception area until he had a moment to spare. She frowned as she took another copy of my resume and led me into the Boardroom.

"It looks like my timing is good," I said, looking around the room at all the empty seats. Half the guys were gone, including the two dark Mediterranean fellows. I could only imagine the scene when Father Zeus gave everyone the lightning bolt in the form of a pink slip and wondered if that was to be my fate as well.

"You're the fifth applicant this week and it's only Tuesday. In fact, you're number three today. It's a bull market," she said, rolling her eyes as if that was the end of the world.

Finally, she opened the door and I went into the wood paneled office. The old man sat at his desk looking surprised to see me. I reached out my hand to shake his and said,

"I want the job."

This made him smile.

"How are you at handling rejection?" he asked. "What if I say no?"

"I'm an expert at cold-calling. I can go right up to a stranger and ask for an order. I don't take any of it personally because I see being a salesman as a role to play, not as myself on trial. I'm exactly the kind of person you're looking for: someone good at cold-calling."

I couldn't believe my own daring and wondered who said those things.

He thought for a moment and cracked a smile.

"You've gotten some coaching since we last met."

"I'm a quick study," I said, not eager to contradict him. "It's a Williams College trait," I added, playing the Athenian alma mater card.

"Tell me, what do you see as your major character fault?"

This standard question is Father Zeus trying to knock Hermes off balance, like when Apollo drags the young god up to Olympus and accuses him of theft. I had to show enough self-awareness to withstand Zeus' scrutiny without being flippant. Hermes was thinking fast.

"I can get a little exuberant," I offered, hoping that was harmless enough.

He sat up alarmed.

"We don't want a loose cannon on deck. This is a professional office."

"My biggest strength is that I actually enjoy dealing with strangers," I threw in.

At this he brightened considerably.

"You're a little sloppy around the edges," he observed, "your tie isn't right, your hair is mussed up, and you're sitting in that chair as though we were old friends."

"We will be," I answered smiling and sitting up straighter. I kept thinking, 'what would Hermes say?' while smiling as he would do, awaiting the assignment from Father Zeus.

He looked pleased.

"I will correct my appearance," I said contritely, "what I have to offer you is someone who will take to cold-calling like a fish to water. I get a kick out of introducing myself to strangers out of the blue. I'm just a naturally outgoing and friendly guy. The key is to remember it's a numbers game and not to take the 'no's personally. New accounts are the lifeblood of this business."

I enjoyed throwing his words back at him. I was humming now in full Hermes and surprising myself with the words coming out of my mouth.

"Tell me more," he said, leaning back in his chair with his hands behind his neck, looking delighted like Zeus meeting his clever son.

"I can make friends in five minutes and it's time to put that skill to work," I said. "I am a natural at getting on someone else's side and seeing things from their point of view. People find me trustworthy because I truly am honest. I'm diligent and will work quickly through the lists."

I kept repeating everything Jim the Preppy Hermes told me, always coming back to "I'm a great cold-caller."

"Love to cold-call," I added simply as he sat considering. The spell was cast.

We sat in silence for almost a minute while I wondered what to do next. I thought if I spoke I might break the spell but then I saw his eyes drifting to the tape on the wall outside his office and I was afraid I'd lose him again to the stream of quotes so I blurted out, "When do I start? You have an empty office now so I know there's a desk for me."

I almost added, "and the gods are with me," but held off, heeding Athena's good judgment.

He brightened at the shove.

"Come back at lunch," he said abruptly, and then, "Noon" before I had a chance to ask him when.

I got on the phone to Jim. He was surprised to hear that I was serious about forsaking Academia and making a living instead.

"I'm converting from Apollo to Hermes," I explained. "Apollo may not mind living in rags, but they don't look good on me."

"You belong in Prada, Banana," he assured me, rhyming the nickname to the designer label. "Just tell him you'll buy lists from Dun and Bradstreet and use the reverse phone directory for the Upper East Side," he said. "I know it's not original but the real money is made by calling the same people everyone else is calling."

He hesitated a moment and then asked, "Are you around this weekend?"

"Sure," I said. I knew he was good for some fun.

When I returned to the office at noon, I found Coffin with a young man with blond hair and blue eyes in a tailored suit looking like he walked off the cover of a fashion magazine. When he looked at me his eyes widened.

"It says here you speak French and German," he told me. "Wolf here speaks German. Speak German to him, Wolf."

Wolf smiled and shook my hand as Coffin went back into his office. He told me he was the boss' desk partner and sat by the secretary, covering his trades when the boss was busy. When I asked him how he was doing he said, "The future looks bright because I'm management material and the old guy can't live forever."

I smiled at the calculating nature behind the angelic demeanor. He presented a darker god, perhaps Apollo the Wolf, out to devour the sheep on other people's pastures. We eyed each other for a moment and I began to sense erotic interest, but Athena's judgment quickly squelched that thought as dangerous and possibly a trap. This was no rube and he might want to fend me off his sacred precinct.

We spoke a few lines about the weather and he seemed satisfied.

"How's his German?" asked Coffin, coming back into the room wearing his suit jacket.

"Pretty good," I answered and they both laughed.

The three of us went downstairs to an Italian restaurant on the corner.

"I presume you eat meat," he said with a wink as he opened the door.

"Paisan, bolognese for three please," Coffin said to the waitress, who obviously knew him. "No time for menus," he told me. "We seldom take lunch. You should be on the phone with your clients while they take lunch and can speak with you."

The food arrived instantly.

"So why do you want to make a lot of money," he asked. "Why not have an easy life at an easy job?"

"You only live once and an easy life doesn't interest me," I told him frankly.

"So what's your magic number: a hundred thousand, two hundred, three hundred a year? What will it take for you to sit back and be happy?"

I gestured as I chewed and swallowed meaningfully.

"I want to become the client," I said.

I could only guess who put those words in my mouth as he laughed and twirled his spaghetti on the spoon.

"We need more hungry guys like you," said Wolf admiringly. "We're putting together a new crew and your timing is perfect."

The waiter came by with dessert but Coffin waved her off.

"Put it on my tab."

It was the fastest lunch I ever ate sitting down.

"Well, my boy," said Coffin, nudging me into the elevator and patting me on the shoulder. "You passed the lunch test."

"What?"

"You know how to use a fork. You don't touch your food with your hands. You eat with your mouth closed. You don't talk with your mouth full. And you don't twirl your spaghetti."

"But *you* twirled your spaghetti," I protested.

"In Italy, everyone twirls his spaghetti," he said, "But we're not in Italy and I've already got a job. We need guys with polish here."

"--or at least a dull sheen," added Wolf.

"So when do I start?" I asked, eager to show him a close. I had the taste of meat in my mouth and I was awaiting my heraldic duties.

"Tomorrow," he said. "Talk to Wolf; he'll give you the details. There's a new class starting every month for rookies and I'm calling established brokers as well."

I shook his hand while looking him firmly in the eye, then let go at just the right moment.

"Thank you, sir," I said, as he made a gesture to walk me towards the elevator, but the secretary caught him by the elbow and said, "Corporates, line 2."

"Be well," he called back to me without turning around.

Back at home I stood before the altar with my arms outstretched exulting in victory.

"Thank you, Hermes," I said, "For showing up when I needed you."

I lit up a joint and headed down to Christopher Street looking for trouble.

Fellow Travellers

Wolf directed me to Security in the basement for clearance, which I presumed was a routine matter. Hermes has to obey the laws of Apollo, who allows him to mislead but not to lie outright. That was the deal they worked out with Zeus that time with the cattle.

The phone rang on the security officer's desk.

"Oh yes," he said, nodding grimly into his hand, "Miss Kore confirms she took cocaine eight to ten times last year, also occasional marijuana use and Xtasy twice. The urine test was positive for all these substances and she admitted only to the marijuana before the tests. So we're going to have to let her go. It would have been another matter if she had owned up beforehand."

I began to panic. I had smoked pot the night before.

"I'll talk to her if I have to," he continued, "but it's pretty much what we've been getting all week."

I was screwed. Here was the purity police from Delphi and I had been a raving Maenad only last night. I wondered if I should confess immediately.

"You're a broker in waiting?" he asked me with an amused lift of the eyebrow. I nodded but could say nothing.

He had me wipe my thumb across an inky spool and press my fingerprint on a file. Then he took my picture and handed me a photo I.D.

"If you lose this call us immediately. We don't want any strangers in the building."

"Is that all?" I asked, my face lighting up.

He gave me a knowing grin.

"Only the support personnel submit to drug tests. Secretaries, operations, people writing checks. We need clean people backing you up. Why, is there any particular test you'd like us to give you?"

He chuckled and stuck his thumbs in his belt.

"We don't test brokers because we need brokers. There aren't a lot of people willing to take the daily abuse you'll be getting without some kind of addiction, sorry to say. And who would ever think of giving a salesman a lie detector test anyway? Only someone who doesn't intend on making any sales. Now get out of here," he finished with gruff affection.

I reported back to Wolf. Again he seemed to be cruising me. I saw his eyes go down a number of times but I was afraid to acknowledge it and kept my eyes glued to his face.

"I manage the new guys," he informed me. "Old Coffin oversees everybody else, so come to me with any trouble-shooting, renegs, that kind of thing."

"What is a reneg?" I asked, figuring there was no advantage now in pretending to know what he was talking about.

"A renegotiation: a scumbag who doesn't pay for the stock," he answered, "You cover the difference when we sell him out. We lose plenty of guys that way."

I pondered the idea of getting fired and owing the firm money as my stomach made a little twitch.

"It's self study for three months, then you take the Series Seven," he told me, leading me toward a conference room off the great floor of desks. "You flunk, you're out. Don't even show up. After that, a week of sales training and practice pitching. You get two thousand a month for six months and then it's straight commission, sink or swim. We've always got a dozen rookies around in different stages of training. Two others started last week: Mal and Messero. Ask the other trainees your questions before you come bug me because I'm busy."

And with that, he turned the knob of the door and gently pushed me in.

"Ok, sharks, here's some fresh meat," he called into the room and disappeared.

"You're the new guy," said one of the frat boys sitting around the conference table in his shirtsleeves.

"Hey everybody!" I smiled, feeling like Apollo the Reject at college again, never quite fitting in with the backslapping Ares types.

"My name is Marilyn, but everyone calls me Mal," said a mousy woman in her forties, standing up to shake my hand officiously. "I'll give you a proper greeting," she said, looking around with disapproval. She looked like a Jewish mother from a sitcom. She was the only woman in the group of young Turks, who were all white except for one Hispanic.

"She's Coffin's daughter-in-law," said the Hispanic guy when she left the room, "and she never shuts the fuck up."

She came back with two coffees.

"This one's for you," she said, smiling unctuously. "I hope you take cream and sugar. There's a cafeteria down the hall."

I thanked her with a look of surprise and pleasure.

"That's one dollar, please," she said, holding out her palm.

"Thank you," I said, fumbling in my pocket.

"There's one other trainee in our class," she said, acting as though she was adopting me. "Mike Messero. He's out this morning at the dentist. He's a big goon."

The others laughed conspiratorially.

"Am I right? You guys know I'm right!"

I frowned. I wondered how I could hide my gayness from these competitive, scrutinizing people.

Messero came in late that afternoon.

I was taken aback by his tremendous size and by the terrible scarring that teenage acne had left on his face, rendering it a roughhewn moonscape. He looked like a sexy Frankenstein, towering at six foot four with the wide shoulders of a football player and bearing the confident stance of a lifelong athlete. His gruff appearance and enormity made him stand out like a sore thumb—and yet he was strangely intriguing, as if in roughing him up the gods had made him rugged, almost worldly, a sort of Sicilian combination of Heathcliff and the Marlboro Man. His dark, ruined skin made him mysterious, for you couldn't help but wonder what suffering he had endured, what interior scarring had occurred under the merciless burden of adolescent disease, and how he had been taunted by his fellow teens who share Artemis' natural cruelty and think nothing of teasing someone twice their size.

And that voice—so deep and macho, and laced with an utterly blue-collar accent straight from the Italian suburbs of Providence! He spat out his words without any distinction between the t's, d's, and th's, and dropping his r's and l's like Elmer Fudd--the classic Providence accent. He looked like he'd been in his share of fights.

I was terrified and fascinated. Here was Ares the War God, tall and butch and defiant. I could only get myself in trouble by opening my overly-refined diction in his vicinity. He would pick up the intellectual tones—the unmistakable 'voice of Apollo' that makes stage voices sound so gay. He'd notice the quick defensive wit and the too-perfect posture. I would be measured in a moment, no doubt, and tormented in a hundred small ways without cease.

I sat at the far corner of the enormous conference desk and avoided his gaze, but it was a losing battle. He had an engaging braggadocio. He loved to compete with the other guys and was comfortable with the inevitable teasing a big brute attracts. He was truly a man's man.

I was not. I hadn't acquired the easy manner of putting my arm around the shoulder of another man in camaraderie. I was so full of Apollo it could only look like romance. I had never excelled in sports even though I liked bodybuilding like so many gay men, and I had never been in a fight in my life.

I clammed up and waited for the right joke to win him over, figuring that Hermes' humor was my best recourse.

Mal gave me the chance, since she was the only woman in the group and she was so outspoken. As she backed into her chair it scraped against the ground, producing a giant fart noise that made everyone look up from his workbook. Mal stared at us with a look of protest.

"It's a talking chair!" she exclaimed, flustered.

"That chair ain't talking!" I jumped in.

At this she reddened and Messero laughed heartily with the rest. I had sparred with the Hera of the group, the Goddess of Manners, so righteous and proper, and had placed myself on the side of Hermes and his love of shocking people. When I had a moment alone with Mal, I apologized.

"Are you kidding?" she said, "I have two boys at home. I'm used to being the only woman with a bunch of guys."

Of course the inevitable icebreaker had to be a scatological joke, the hallmark of Hermes, the smelly babe who poops in dignified Apollo's arms that time with Zeus.

After work I ran into Messero by the elevator.

"Walk with me to the World Trade Center," he said, half inviting and half commanding, pronouncing it *da Wo Trate Cennuh*.

How could I say no to this big sexy galoot? We walked in silence for a few blocks. I was too nervous to speak, afraid my gayness would announce itself through a casual remark or gesture.

As we neared the entrance, a large black man bumped into Messero.

"Hey whatchit, asshole," he barked.

"What you call me?" asked the man, who was as big as him.

"C'mon," I said, pulling him by the arm. "You have to pick your fights carefully."

"He bumped into me on purpose."

"Who cares?" I said, relieved when we entered the building surrounded by people in suits. I didn't need Ares stirring up a fight over nothing, but I couldn't help admire the courage that the god gave him. As long as Athena's judgment is there to guide his actions, that aggressiveness is a trait for success.

"You look like you work out a bit, though you're not in that great a shape," he told me, assessing my physique through my suit.

"I've been running lately."

"You gotta do more weights. Your proportions are good but you need more in your shoulders and back."

"You must work out every day," I said, admiringly. I was careful not to let him hear me sigh.

"Yep. These guys who say they're too busy to work out are full of shit. They all got an hour of T.V. they could sacrifice. Most of them don't even try. They just get big and fat sitting on their ass all day chasing bucks."

We stopped at a coffee stand while he got a cup. I could see a speech formulating in his mind.

"Man's endeavors boil down to a hunt for pussy," he said, assuming a philosophical tone. "If you make an okay living and take care of yourself, you'll probably get pussy. If you make a lot of money, it doesn't matter what you look like. The pussy will find its way to you. The Jaguar convertible with a babe in it always has some ugly guy with a belly and swollen eyes at the wheel. It's because he's got something big and fat bulging in his pants, meaning his wallet."

"So you came downtown for the pussy?" I said, stammering out the last word uncomfortably.

"I don't just want money, Jack. I want to have it all."

"And what's having it all?" I asked, girding myself.

"Oh that's easy," he said, eagerly taking the bait. "To have it all a guy's got to have four things. One, he's got to have dough, as I said. Two, he's got to be tall. Three, he's got to be dahk. And Four, he's got to have a big dick."

I considered the Messero Manifesto as he looked around proudly to see if anyone else was listening.

"Hey," he said, nudging me with a sly grin, "Three out of four ain't bad."

I watched Messero disappear into the mob flowing down the escalator to the PATH train, wondering if I had been come onto or not. His homo-eros was undeniable but this man was straight. He liked men and disliked women except as lovers and the Eternal Feminine. If he obviously liked to be admired by other men it didn't make him gay, it only made him Italian.

Of course Eros had my knees shaking. He was so masculine I would've jumped if he told me to, and I couldn't help thinking about his body. Just let him get drunk one night and complain about his girlfriend, I thought, and I'd be waiting in the wings. But chances are he gets what he wants or he walks away.

Yes, he was a goon, but he was such a very big goon.

"Come work out wid me and the guys," he told me the next day in the cafeteria where we started studying to get away from the crowded room and Mal's incessant chatter.

The next day I brought my gym bag.

Messero flirted with the woman at the front desk, repeating her name coyly while I waited behind him clutching my bag.

"Broads love the sound of their names," he explained later.

In the locker room, I was treated to a full view of his physique, the body of Ares himself.

"All natural, too," he said, making a bicep and drinking up my looks. "I do look pretty good, don't I?" he asked, checking himself out in the mirror and doing the chest pose. This was not the stare of Narcissus; this was the critical glance of the bodybuilder who searches for faults as he scans the vast stretches of muscle for something to improve. He made a triceps.

"I love the gym," he said, exulting. "It's where I feel at home. My neighborhood in Cranston was all guys. The gym was where I spent my yoot."

"How could your neighborhood be all guys?" I asked, starting to feel comfortable enough to challenge him. "Where were the women?"

"In the kitchen," he laughed. He was standing in his jock strap while I sat on the wooden bench beside him at cock level. I tried not to look but he stood there all but naked and talked to me through the mirror while my peripheral vision, honed through long hours of practice at gay bars, worked furiously.

"It's just as well," he continued, "because men and women can't be just friends. You can be lovers. You can fuck. But you can't be just friends."

"My best friends are women," I ventured and immediately regretted opening myself up to further inspection.

"Yeah, buddy, no offense but you're the urbane kind of guy who likes women that way. You're not the macho man type."

"You mean I'm effete."

"I don't know aboutcha feet," he answered laughing, "But you're polished and I mean that in a good way. Women like being friends with a guy like you because you're not a threat to them. With me, it's sex or nothing and I'm fine with that. Sit on my face or get out of my face."

"Don't you go through sexual dry spells?" I asked, eager to spot a need.

"Put it this way, if I walk in the door and we aren't tearing each other's clothes off and having sex on the floor then we've got a problem. I don't want one of those English marriages."

"You want to get married?"

"Who's asking?" he answered. I almost choked.

"I'm not the marrying kind," he continued. "I've got too much wanderlust," a word he pronounced with great reverence. "I want to spread my seed around."

We started with the bench press. My first set I lifted one hundred thirty-five pounds for ten reps, which is one big plate on either side.

"This is just a warm up," he said, jumping into my spot and pumping out twenty fast ones, his face changing to angry Ares as soon as his hands touched the iron.

"Don't worry about the weight," he assured me as he doubled it, "and I'm not just bustin' bawls."

"I'll be lucky to do one rep at 225."

"You're not ready to do any at this weight yet," he answered with authority.

As he pushed his limits he heaved his chest and groaned like an animal. Now I knew what he sounded like having an orgasm. A few of the guys working out near us looked up at the rack of plates like admiring soldiers.

Next to this giant I was Jack in the Beanstalk. I was fascinated. Lifting weight gave him Ares' courage through the burn in the muscle and the fighting grunt of the heavy lift. I had to stick around this guy and the weight room if I wanted that courage.

He lay down on the bench as I spotted him from behind his head.

"Working out wid a guy is as close as you can get without getting quee-ah," he said sprawling below me. "Take the bench press. You gotcha face in a guy's smelly crotch with all the sweat dripping down and you can see up his shorts where he's hanging. It's bizz-aah."

"What do you think of Mal," I asked, panicking for a new direction to the conversation. My erection was stirring.

"Little Jewish Mama came down to Wall Street to make some money. We had lunch first week of training. She makes you listen to how she has to get her kids excused from the Pledge of Allegiance, how her son wants to go to public high school but she makes him go to schul, how he wants to be an athlete but she's worried about injuries. I have to listen to her tell me all the fine points of kosher food and porcelain, how her friends had a terrible time when they went to Germany, and so I ask her, 'why does a Jew go to Germany?' Her answer was, "sprechen Sie Deutsch, droppen Sie dead.'"

"She's a tough bird, though," I said, "and maybe she'll make it." I was trying to adopt his diction.

"She won't last six months," he answered. "She only got in because she's married to old Coffin's son. She's not a survivor, she's too personal about everything."

He got up from the bench, his voice slipping back into philosophical mode, "There's no such thing as a happy woman. There's always something. 'I'm depressed.' 'Why?' 'I don't know.' There's always something. You will never in your life hear a woman say, 'Gee, I feel happy today.'"

"Life is tragic, I guess."

"We all got dealt a bad hand. With Mal, you combine the fact that's she's an ugly broad and that tragic Jewish history, so guaranteed bad ending. And she'd rather be right than happy anyday so she's never going to smile unless it's sarcasm."

This man was a combination of Ares and Hermes. He was as eager to dominate as to charm. Ares always had a problem with his mother Hera, with her love of society and personal feelings. Ares doesn't need other people's approval like she does. He does what he wants to do.

But several times when the others were distracted I had caught Messero staring down at the table with his face dropped. The moment he felt my gaze Athena's shield went up and he resumed his professional mien, but there was always something stoic and resigned under the working class veneer, a jaded courage that doesn't look back but moves on, silently carrying its poignant memories along with it. He seemed the kind of guy you could tell anything to. I wondered how many friends he kept.

"So you're Italian?" I asked after another set of dumbbell presses.

"Italian and Knuk," he answered, making a bicep in the mirror. "What do you think?" he asked, lifting up his tank top and showing me his back, which formed an enormous cobra V.

I approved guardedly, not wanting to show too much interest, although I knew he was playing with me and was pretty sure he had me figured out.

'I'm not at all proud of the French part," he said, "Bunch of snobs and cheap asses. I like the Italian side, all passion and secrets."

We went into the shower together. I was aching everywhere and eager to run away before my erection crept up but then I found myself in the group shower with this naked Herakles. I turned my back as I dropped my towel and put the water down cold.

"How much do you weigh?" I asked when he caught me staring.

"Two twenty-nine and all muscle except for about five pounds of this," he said, grabbing his soapy member. "If my quads weren't so huge this would look even bigger."

"So you have no trouble getting what you want?" I asked, immediately regretting my indiscretion.

"Are you kidding?" he said, "They gag all night."

The next morning, Messero fired the opening salvo. He was an Ares out to get everyone's goat.

"So doesn't Snyder look like a Hasid with a Land's End makeover?" he asked the group.

"I don't think Gary looks Jewish," said Mal.

"No one thinks I'm Jewish," said Snyder, offended.

"What's so bad about looking Jewish," asked Messero, egging them on.

"I think he's very WASPy," said Mal.

"And I say he looks like a Jew," said Messero indignantly. "How could anyone ever take him for English? Sure he's got the Weejuns and Tattersalls but he sure doesn't look like he grew up sailing. He hasn't got an athletic bone in his body and his nose goes around the corner ten seconds before his head shows up."

"Why are you picking on my nose?" demanded Snyder. "You should talk with that schnozz."

"Oh there's that lovely language again," said Messero, stirring the pot.

"No one ever thinks I'm Jewish either," said Mal.

At this the room erupted.

"You look like you walked off the set of 'Fiddler on the Roof.'"

"I am often taken for Italian."

"Eye-talian! You think you look like me?" he demanded, feigning outrage.

"I didn't say big ugly stupid Italian. Northern Italian."

"You don't look like any Italian I ever met."

"Have you ever met any from the upper classes?" she asked. This got a big cheer.

"My point," said Messero when we got quiet again, "is that no Jew wants to look like a Jew."

"Jewish person," said Mal. "At least be polite."

"Why do I have to add 'person' to it?" he demanded. "I don't say English person or French person. Aren't we all talking about persons here?"

"It's 'people' not 'persons' and you're a moron," she said, "There's a history behind it," she added more solemnly.

"Mike, chill," I said. I had enough Athena in me to sense we had come up against a line and enough Hermes to know that ethnic teasing is only funny when there's good will behind it.

"No one should be insulted," he answered. "So why do you all get nose jobs?"

"I didn't get a nose job," said Snyder.

"Mal did," said Messero, "didn't you Mal, or did you get that Julie Andrews nub from your mother?"

Mal looked down, reddening.

"Mike," I insisted, "you shouldn't talk about noses."

"Yeah," joined Snyder, "It's the biggest one in the room."

We were all back in good humor and enjoying the sparring.

"You know what they say about big noses," said Marzaro.

"Yeah," said Mal, "Big noses, little dicks."

The boys roared at this profanity from the little matron.

"You're the Big Nose around here," I said, looking at all the engaged faces.

"He is just one big nose," said Mal with a smile.

--"so we'll call you Big Nose," I concluded triumphantly, safely ensconced in Hermes the Frat-Boy.

"Aw, no nicknames," he said, shaking his head, used to being a Sore Thumb.

"Big Nose, Big Nose, Big Nose," we chanted until he left the room.

The name stuck for the rest of his career. I considered it a personal triumph. I had branded him like Hermes putting a sticker on a sales item. Nicknames always pop up when Hermes is around because they make people exchangeable. And I knew from Williams that the best nicknames like Chip, Skip, and Bud have nothing to do with your actual name.

Big Nose began studying away from the crowd in the cafeteria, which had the same spectacular view of Battery Park as the Boardroom and was empty most of the day. I sat a few seats away to prevent our eyes from meeting and inciting unnecessary conversation. Apollo was in charge while we studied for our exams, so there was no time for Hermes and his diversions.

One late afternoon I became aware of a young Chinese man staring at me from across the room. His face was gaunt and he leered at me with what could only be sexual interest. When he winked at me brazenly behind Big Nose's back, I knew he was a sordid Eros on the make.

He wasn't from the Boardroom. I looked away but couldn't help checking him out again and again, because Apollo's studying makes most people long for a physical connection. Always he met my eyes behind Big Nose, who seemed oblivious of our interaction.

He showed up in the cafeteria every day thereafter, staring outrageously from the other side of the room. Utterly distracted, I couldn't believe his blatant daring in the most heterosexual milieu in the city.

Finally, he came over to us one morning.

"You're brokers in training?" he asked. "I'm Manny. I'm going to be a trader."

His voice was deep and crisp, another virtue the Greeks considered a gift of the gods.

"Hutton is setting me up with a trading account at the Eurodollar desk," he explained.

Big Nose was intrigued.

"How does that work?" he asked. "Do you have to look for clients?"

"No, they give you a certain amount of money and it's your baby, win or lose. If you make winning trades, you keep a percentage; if you lose, you're fired and you can even wind up owing the firm money. There's a two-year ulcer, they warn us, so I'm hoping to get in a good five years with proper medication. A friend of mine made one little miscalculation and lost out a year's work in a single day. If she'd called in sick that day, she would've been made. Instead she's in the hole and unemployed on top of it."

"She?" asked Big Nose.

"Math whiz," he answered.

"That sounds better than being a broker," said Big Nose, "because then you're free in five years to do something else."

"Doesn't studying make you horny?" asked Manny out of the blue.

I agreed.

"I sit here with a hard on and want to get off somehow," he continued brazenly.

Big Nose stared out at the Harbor.

"I was at Harry's the other day and this guy was in the men's room sucking another guy off."

"At Harry's?" asked Big Nose.

"When he was done I let him suck me off, too," he said, looking right at me. "A mouth's a mouth."

I nodded cautiously, caught up in the Centaur's lust that disregards society.

"What are you both crazy?" asked Big Nose. "That's disgusting. Sloppy seconds from some gay guy?"

"Yeah, Manny," I interrupted, trying to recoup. "Spare us the gory details."

When he left, Big Nose said, "I can't believe you went along with him."

"You get more details if you don't act surprised."

"So you fished him in," he said appreciatively.

I said nothing.

"I don't care if you're gay," he added suddenly.

My heart raced.

"You're the most heterosexual guy I've ever met," I told him, trying to flatter my way out of a corner. I did not bother to contradict him but I didn't dare admit anything either. I could get fired if that ever got out.

Manny didn't show up in the cafeteria for a week after that. The next time I saw him, he didn't come into the room. He peered around the corner at me out of sight of Big Nose and nodded towards the stairwell. Then he slipped through the door.

It was three in the afternoon and I was crazed with boredom and horniness. I excused myself to go to the bathroom.

Manny was kneeling a couple of stairs down with his mouth wide open.

"You don't have to act like such a weirdo," I whispered, unzipping.

"Do you want it or not?"

This was a *hermaion,* a gift from Hermes, sneaked in a stairwell and stolen from a day of work. I thrilled at the illicit situation and the tension made it all go swiftly.

"Meet me here every day at two and we can do it for the next two weeks till I start trading."

"Don't talk so loud," I told him, looking around afraid.

I ran into the men's room to wash my face and calm down.

In the mirror, I checked out a sore area on my tongue that had been bothering me for days. There was a small white spot on the side the size of a grain of rice.

"Jesus, its candidiasis," I said to my reflection, citing one of the early symptoms of AIDS.

I couldn't have AIDS. Only sleazy guys who did heavy drugs and had multiple partners got AIDS. I was seldom on the bottom and mostly stuck to oral sex, which was supposed to be safe. But I had seen a slim young man changing into a suit in the locker room at the gym with purple marks on his legs who didn't look sleazy at all. When he saw me staring he frowned and I looked away.

I felt a cloud descend around my shoulders. I didn't have time for health issues, never mind AIDS.

I stuck out my tongue again. Then I pinched the spot between my fingernails until it broke off, leaving a droplet of blood.

I smiled into the mirror.

"Nonsense," I told my reflection, and looked again and again.

The Art of Sales

I sat with Mal and Big Nose in a hotel conference hall with a hundred trainees from around the country to hear the famous sales lectures by Dick Ward, Master of Intangible Sales. The room was full of aspiring Hermes, three men to every woman and all very enthusiastic, for they had each been drawn to the god as I had been, having come to the conclusion that it takes money to live the Good Life, and that the Good Life is the only one worth living.

Dick walked on stage precisely on time—he must have been standing behind the door looking at his watch--and did a little strut in his black Bostonians, the kind with the little punctured holes, greeting members of the audience with many hello's and waves of the hand, making brief eye contact with as many of us as he could. He was Black Irish with piercing blue eyes, fair skin, and jet black hair. His slender, nimble physique could only come from a sport like running or wrestling, with his Gucci suit clinging to an intriguing bulge.

"Hello trainees," he said, stopping downstage and holding out his arms in greeting. "Say, hello Dick," he commanded.

"Hello, Dick," we roared back.

"I just love hearing that," he nodded theatrically.

"I got my nice treads on for youse guys today," he started, exaggerating the New Yorkese for the out-of-towners. Then he switched, "But if you're smart, it won't matter what you're wearing because this business, if conducted properly, is a telephone business. It's telemarketing, only instead of selling subscriptions you're selling hopes and dreams in the form of financial securities."

"First things first. Keep your personal problems to yourself. Be cheerful; look cheerful. No one buys from a grumpy puss; leave that to the insurance guys with their what-will-you-do's. You need to create a sales persona and stick with it because that's the person who's going to succeed. When you go home tonight start thinking about what that guy or that gal is like. Write a nice long paragraph about your sales persona, print it up, and tape a picture from a magazine on it and stick it on your fridge so you can greet him or her and start getting acquainted. That's the person the client is going to meet and who's going to make you rich."

"The trick is to keep it real at the same time," he said, holding up an admonishing finger. "Be personable, not personal. Be friendly, not friends. Be likeable, but don't be yourself."

A snicker worked its way through the audience.

"Mr. and Mrs. Jones can buy stocks and bonds from anyone so you have to give them a reason to buy them from you and not from the other guy. They've got to like you and the best way to be liked is to pretend you like them and you're already friends. Admire them in some way--or make them think you do—and they'll automatically like you back. Your goal is to become a mirror to the client so he can project right into it."

With that he paused and became reverent.

"Confidence sells. Enthusiasm sells. But confidence isn't something you are born with—with a few exceptions--" and at this he did one quick, comic pelvic thrust that elicited a few screams from the women, followed by general laughter, "confidence is something that's out there that you tap into. The word means 'with faith' so there's nothing personal about it."

He let this sink in for a moment.

"I'm sure many of you never thought you were going to wind up as a salesman. A salesman? The first thing you think of is some asshole kicking tires in a used car lot."

He looked around the room nodding and repeating softly, "Am I right? Am I right?"

"The dignity of sales comes from the product," he resumed. "There's nothing to be embarrassed about selling jet planes at the Paris Air Show. When you believe in what you're selling, a sales job is a profession. So don't buy junk or gimmicks. Buy only A-rated stocks like JNJ and Coca Cola and build a solid basis for wealth for your clients and for yourself. Then you're not taking advantage of anyone. You're not a con artist. You're providing a needed service."

I awed at the presence of the god with his easy manner and demeanor.

"You'll get confidence for free if you believe in your product and know the details back and forth. Don't get on the phone until you're fully armed and loaded. You need a growth stock, a dividend stock, a Dow stock, a stock under thirty, a stock under ten, and a stock in the news. Get stories and numbers to back them up all like, 'Mr. Jones, Harley Davidson is selling motorcycles to retiring Boomers' or, 'Mr. Jones, JNJ has raised its dividend for twenty-five years in a row and there's no end in sight.' Have a few bonds up your sleeve as well: one taxable, one tax-free, and a zero-coupon. Zeroes are good for new clients because it makes them feel rich already to buy a ten thousand dollar maturity for seven thousand dollars. Their statements will work the magic for you."

"It's not your job to make the guy a fortune or to be a genius. Leave that to the bald guys on t.v. Your job is just to keep the client. If he loses money in something he never heard of until you came along then he's not going to stick around for more. If he's down a few points in JNJ or Pepsi or Pillsbury he'll stay, so don't try to be the Wizard of Wall Street."

"The key is to ask questions. Whoever asks the questions controls the conversation. Listen to the guy and figure out exactly what he needs, because you've got some of that. You're not here to foist ideas on him. You're here to supply the right investment for his needs and his risk tolerance. You cold-call with a specific idea but that's really just to bounce something off of him to find out what he actually needs. It's like hunting: you may go out looking for deer but the woods are full of rabbit so that's what you're having for dinner tonight."

The idea of eating the client for dinner garnered a few chuckles.

"When a guy's got money, *No* never means *no*. It means you haven't listened close enough. He may just need a CD and that's fine even though there's no commission in it, because one day that CD will come due and he'll trust you by then and you'll have something sexier waiting for his say-so."

"Now with the questions, some of you may think you're being nosy, but does the doctor act embarrassed when he asks about your hemorrhoids? You're the doctor and the client is the patient. You need to ask questions because everyone has a different idea of what it means to be 'conservative' or 'aggressive'. Some folks think a five-year bond is way too sexy. Sends chills down their spine. Ask questions and listen patiently. Never interrupt a client—and there are no exceptions to that one rule!"

We nodded collectively. He had us in the palm of his hand.

"You're all young and that's a point against you with middle aged investors, but if there's no way out and you do have to go meet him, invite him to your office. That way you'll have the institutional stage to back up your youth. And when he comes in don't receive him sitting behind your desk. Get out in front of your desk and shake his hand standing up and looking him in the eye. Don't seat him across from your desk, seat him beside you so you're on the same side physically and you can see each other's bodies. That creates trust."

He paused.

"And that way you can pick his pocket."

We laughed. The room was like a single person that he was relating to with the comfort of an old friend. Mal and Big Nose were as enraptured as I was.

"Look for physical signs that the guy is ready to close. As long as he's got his arms folded, he's dwelling in his mountain fortress, so wait until he relaxes and drops his arms, then go for the close."

"If his fists are clenched, he's hanging onto his money in his mind, so keep the questions coming and listen to what he says and adjust your product as necessary. When his fists loosen up, go for the close."

"If he's rubbing his chin or stroking his nose, it means *enough facts,* so go for the close."

"If he sighs audibly, he's telling you he's ready so go for the close."

"And if he starts picking up any documents you brought with you--a margin agreement or a W-9--skip the close and help him fill out the forms because you've already closed. If you keep force-feeding him facts you'll kill the sale."

Dick's charm was undeniable. He was completely poised and relaxed. I was taking notes as fast as I could.

His constant vacillation between different attitudes transfixed the crowd. He went from deadpan to smirk to smile instantly, like a dog waking up barking. Dick's roguish blue eyes enjoyed the admiration and lust from the crowd of twenty five year old's. He was in the prime of life with a slender waist and hints of muscle that leaned through his suit. And then of course there was that intriguing bulge in his Gucci suit.

"The key to selling," he said, his voice reverent again, "is to become the parent. First off, pronounce the guy's name correctly. Blow that and it's over. If it's a weird name and you aren't sure, ask around before you make the call. People like the sound of their names. Their parents used their names, so say them over and over during the conversation. Sprinkle it in naturally, 'Mr. Jones. You see, Mr. Jones, this idea is just right for your objectives. I am perfectly comfortable with this investment for you, Mr. Jones.'"

His facility with role-play was very sexy. 'Who was Dick Ward?' I wondered. I saw the same fascination and admiration on Messero's face.

Mal was in love with the guy, glowing and looking down smiling.

"Everyone out there in T.V. Land is looking for Big Daddy," he continued, straightening up on the edge of the stage. "No one knows how to make sense of life now that the religions are gone and there's nothing to believe in. Chances are your best clients—people in their fifties—have lost their parents and there's no Big Daddy left to tell them what to do. They're lost in the city and all the guidebooks and maps have been tossed out the window."

"They're bereft," he said looking up comically. Then he pointed one foot and tipped his shoe left and right.

"If you can fill size twelve shoes you'll make millions. People are terrified out there and they want security. You sell securities. It's a lot easier to face the Void with a nice, dividend-producing portfolio backing you up. You can take comfort in a thousand shares of Coca Cola, and a million dollar in bonds works better than a sleeping pill for those late nights tossing and turning."

We nodded collectively.

"Talk to them. Find out what the Big Dream is so you can frame the investment around it. 'This stock portfolio is your house on the Sound, Mr. Jones. It's your retirement, Mr. Jones, your education for your kids.' Remind them why they need to invest. 'This is a down payment on that thirty-foot sailboat, Mr. Jones.'"

"You don't need to have natural charm or personality if you can pretend you do. It's all in the air so just breathe some in. You have the same brain as the guy who has charisma. If you're not brave, don't be brave. Let the sales persona be brave for you. Leave yourself out of it. Pretending is as easy as putting on clothes."

He gave us a mischievous look. The audience tittered. Suddenly he started wiggling his hips and taking off his jacket slowly and tossed it on the stage as little shrieks from the women in the group accented his every move. He unbuttoned his shirt as we began clapping in unison. He played to us, slowly pulling off his shirt with many false starts and then tossing it on the floor, with his undershirt soon to follow.

The hard body rippled with washboard abs under the stage lighting. We were all shouting. Then he turned his back to us and gestured as if undoing his pants while we egged him on. To our amazement, he kicked his shoes into the crowd and dropped his pants, standing in red silk boxers with his back to us.

Then he turned around to face the now boisterous room and did a few hip checks to unheard music, his penis neatly outlined down one side of his boxers. Suddenly he stopped and his face looked serious again.

"So check your closet," he continued at the edge of the stage, holding out his hands to silence us. "The size twelve shoes are in there somewhere. Maybe an uncle you used to fear and respect, maybe your dad or a teacher, an old boss, or a priest or rabbi. Someone in your life was Big Daddy so put him on when you shower and get dressed in the morning and wear him until you get home, because he's the one who's going to be assertive and can handle the abuse and the worry and the uncertainty that comes with this profession."

He seemed utterly un-self conscious standing almost naked before us. Messero winked at me and said, "The guy's in great shape," as Mal blushed and shook her head.

"Use the lower range of your voice. Most people walk around using their adolescent voice, talking in the upper range because they're afraid to assert anything. Remember, up-speak never makes a sale."

"Now everyone, say the word *no* as if you were yelling at a dog who's about to step out on the street in front of a car."

"No."

"That's Big Daddy's voice. That's the voice they'll trust and believe, so cultivate it. It's your real voice, not your apologetic voice, not your teenage voice. Get to know that voice and start using that voice. No one will challenge it because it's authentic, so make it second nature and lose that flute you've been blowing on for years."

We cackled. He did another hip check, back in stripper persona.

"Blow that flute, baby," he growled. The women screamed.

"Modulate your voice," he continued, looking serious again. "Let it go up and down to show emotion because authentic emotion sells and it will reel him in. Make it personal for the client but don't let it be personal for you."

"Tell them once, tell them twice. You cast the spell with repetition. When you get the order repeat the price objective. 'Mr. Jones, we are buying Alcoa at 7 and holding for 10 dollars a share.' That way everyone's clear on what is happening and the last thing he hears is that he's already making a profit."

"You may be uncomfortable playing Big Daddy at first, but that's what you are paid for. You are paid to be uncomfortable. Just tell yourself, 'I'm uncomfortablo doing this' and then do it anyway. Do you think I was born comfortable standing in front of strangers on stage in my underwear?"

We all shouted and whistled at this cue.

"Do you think?" he baited us, turning around and wiggling his hard buttocks, then turning back again.

"When a stock is down you're going to feel uncomfortable. But don't wait for Mr. Jones to call you first. Big Daddy always calls first when there's bad news and the short term trade turns into a long term hold."

We groaned.

"Calling him before he calls you takes the wind out of his sails. Let him be angry. Let him rant until he feels foolish. If you interrupt a client you put yourself on the other side."

"When he's finished bitching use his complaint to ask a 'yes' question. 'Mr. Jones, Pepsi is down ten points.' 'Yes.' 'And you're worried and surprised.' 'Yes.' 'It's a beautiful day out, isn't it?' 'Yes.' 'And you hate my guts at the moment.' 'Yes.'"

"You're good as long as he keeps saying 'yes' because that word works like a whammy on his brain."

"Now for the next move. If you liked Pepsi at fifty, you should be all over it at forty, right? Get him to double up, 'because this is a unique opportunity, Mr. Jones, and we already know the stock is capable of going to fifty.'"

We chuckled at his logic. Big Nose jabbed me with his elbow.

"It's not his anger you have to worry about, my friends," he continued. "It's his silence. You can work with 'fuck you'. You gotta worry when he doesn't call you back. Now if he's poor and you bury him, be a sport and go pick on someone else. But if he's got money, he's got money to lose. Your job is to make sure he loses it with you and not with someone else."

At this the room laughed heartily.

"Now, closing. When in doubt, go for the close because that will uncover the objection. The key to closing is to take the choice away from the client. Never ask a 'yes' or 'no' question. Never ask him if he wants to buy the stock. Don't treat him like a simpleton. You just have to help him with the decision by making it with him. 'Mr. Jones, I want you to own a thousand shares; let's start with a thousand shares; let's move in on a thousand shares; let's own a thousand shares.' Notice that magic word, *let's*. Or maybe, 'Mr. Jones, are you in a position to do a thousand shares or do you want to start with five hundred shares at forty dollars a share? We'll buy another five hundred at fifty after the earnings come out, etc.'"

"Avoid using the word 'stock'. You're not selling stocks; you're selling dreams."

"Now his greatest weapon is, 'I want to think about it.' The cure for that is urgency. Add it like spice. Let him know he'll lose out if he waits. 'Mr. Jones, I'm very comfortable with this investment for you; it's what you need, Mr. Jones, and now is the right time to own it; you've got to be in it to win it; you don't have to think about it because all the thinking has been done already. Our experts at the firm have fully vetted this investment and they are strongly recommending action at these price levels'—and 'these price levels' covers you if it goes down a point or two before the check clears. 'Mr. Jones, I want to make a significant difference in your lifestyle.'"

We burst out laughing.

"You see the guy in rags?"

He began walking in mock stealth in a little circle on the stage, his silky boxers clinging to his impeccable physique.

"Don't confront the giant directly. You've got to step around Goliath and avoid the 'yes' and 'no'. State a positive action that is not a choice. 'You won't have to lose any sleep about this investment, Mr. Jones. I am building a position with all my clients in this investment, Mr. Jones, and I will tell you when to sell and take the profits. Let's take advantage of this outstanding opportunity, Mr. Jones'."

"*Let's* is your best friend because it *let's* him off the hook."

He looked at his watch.

"Okay, to summarize, go for the close and when he objects, repeat the objection so he says the word *yes*, then answer the objection and go for the close again. When you don't know what to do, go for the close. The guy who asks for the order wins."

He picked up his pants and pulled them on, leaving the buckle of his belt open. Then he stood at the edge of the stage directly under the down light so his abs cut up like an athletic model as he opened his arms in exhortation.

"Go for the close and then shut the fuck up. Whoever talks first loses. Let the uncomfortable silence enter the conversation like a thief reaching into his pocket. Look at your phone, twirl your hair, or scratch your balls—just don't speak because now you have him cornered. I've spent a full minute staring at my watch and waiting for a sound from the other end of the line."

He put his shirt back on and tucked it in.

"There's an answer to every objection. If he says 'the price is too high' tell him 'that's what stocks that go up look like, Mr. Jones'. Then go for the close and shut the fuck up."

He slipped his tie around his neck and tied a loose knot as the room remained captivated in silence. Then he pointed at the women who caught his shoes when he kicked them off his feet and invited them up on the stage. He shook their hands warmly and put on his shoes as they climbed back off the stage, delighted.

"Remember: there's one bright side to when things go wrong and everything's down."

We waited.

"It's not your money."

We looked at each other in glee. His ability to work the group was amazing. His psychological fluidity was a mystery and a gift--the way he threw in little voices and faces as if he was changing masks right before our eyes.

I was the first one with questions when he opened the floor.

"We have to tell the truth, but can we say 'this stock is going up' even though we don't know, we only hope that it does?"

"Absolutely," he answered. "You've got to take a stand. You can't lie or say you have inside information, but you can state the future with confidence. 'This stock is going through the roof, Mr. Jones, and you have to own it'. And remember, every stock is either a buy or a sell. Holding is the road to starvation, unless the guy has more funds to capture."

He looked at his watch again. We were getting tired As the Greeks would say, Hermes had entered the room.

"Sad to say, your first accounts are sacrificial lambs for the better accounts to come. Hey, they said *yes* didn't they? Do you tell everyone you sleep with that you have herpes when you're not in the middle of an outbreak? What were they doing out at three in the morning anyway? It's a dangerous world, baby, especially at nighttime."

He gave a whistle. This was the warning Hermes gave the turtle he found outside his door, right before he took him inside and stabbed him viciously with a knife, scooping out his insides to get his first taste of meat.

"Now let me say a few things about being a woman in this business, because I see a lot of nice looking young women in this group and that's a growing trend on the Street. Every single one of you women is a pioneer and a women's libber in the most important sense--making money. Real change doesn't come from marching in the streets demanding rights but by climbing up the corporate ladder, so I commend each and every one of you."

"The women in this business eat nails for breakfast. You need to turn your sex to your advantage, because a middle-aged guy with money and misery at home might just like having a financial affair over the phone."

"So talk in a low voice. Get him to confide in you. Be his therapist and the other woman and the femme fatale who happens to have a stock idea that will solve his problems, at least the ones that money can help. If he tells a dirty joke, laugh along with him—just don't sleep with him, because you've already got him by the balls and while your hand is in his pocket, you can grab his wallet."

He pointed at Mal.

"What's your name, young lady?" he asked with no hint of irony.

"Mal," she answered, flustered, "and thank you very much."

"So Mal, do you take milk and sugar with your nails or do you eat them dry right out of the box?"

"Right out of the box," she quipped. "A girl's got to watch her weight."

"That's what I'm talking about," he shouted. "Just throw it right back at him and you control the situation. You can trip the guy with his own weight using humor like Mal just did."

"I've got 3 sons at home," she interjected.

"So you've seen your share of The Three Stooges."

"Oh my god," she laughed, putting her face in her hands.

"You know how easy guys are to manipulate. Once you get comfortable with him, start in on how concerned you are about his future and how you can make a difference."

"Now everyone go to lunch," he announced abruptly and walked off stage with our applause.

We were told to find a stock to use for role-playing for a week. I pitched GE ("In business for over a century") and stumbled through my first few dozen calls because I was too self-conscious, but once I reminded myself that 'this is Hermes calling' everything changed quickly.

"Cold calling is like sticking your face in a cheese grater," Dick told us. "Keep doing it until there's no Ego left to grate away, which is fine because Egos make terrible salespeople. Mirrors make great salespeople. Remember, you can't have your cake and eat it too, but you *can* eat someone else's cake."

As an exercise in getting out of ourselves, he had us practice pitching using funny voices and accents. Everyone had a few up his sleeve. It is a Hermes trait.

Big Nose did a great Fred Flintstone and somehow lost his accent while Mal made a high pitched girly squeak like a flapper.

I pulled up a few funny voices from my clowning-around days in high school.

Dick was pleased.

"Okay, I'm fifty and I own an auto-body shop so I'm blue collar with a couple of hundred thousand in passbook savings. I probably have an account at Schwab because I'm a self-help kind of guy. Go."

I dialed an imaginary number on one of the dead phones scattered around the room. I went with an exaggerated Southern accent.

"Joe's Auto-body, can I help you?"

Dick was talking like Bullwinkle the Moose. I couldn't help laughing.

"Can I help you?" he repeated.

"Hello, yes, may Ah speak to the owner ple-ahz?"

"That's me and I don't like the sound of this. Either you're unhappy with something or you're selling me something."

"I'm going to double your money in five yee-ahs," I said.

"The only idea I'm interested in right now is can you help me find a new mechanic. I got three cars waiting and my guy don't know shit about Jaguars." He ditched Bullwinkle and went back to New Yorkese.

"I cayan't help you fix y'all's Jaguar, but I can help you buy your very own little old Jaguar," I quipped in Southern Belle, and then reverted to my normal voice, afraid of how effeminate it sounded. "I'm calling from C.F. I lutton because I believe Jaguar is going to be taken over by one of the Big Three automakers and I want you to be a part of that. As you know, the waiting list is six months. The stock is at half its growth rate and it's a turnaround story—"

"You know what happens when you turn around?"

"You get rear-ended," I answered. Hermes put the words in my mouth.

He laughed.

"Well I do happen to like Jaguar," he said, opening for me.

"Let's move in on one thousand shares at twenty four dollars a share. In five years we'll break out the champagne in your new car."

"In five years I could be dead."

"Then your kids will be twice as rich."

"Are you guaranteeing this?" he asked, testing.

"I only sell what I believe in."

"I've got a broker."

He was throwing everything at me. That was a good sign. Zeus had Hermes on his lap.

"But you don't hayave me," I answered, back in Southern Belle.

He responded in Foghorn Leghorn, "Oh, Ah do detect—Ah say, Ah do detect the slahtest note of conceit, Suh."

"I'm onto something and I want you in it, Mr. Jones," I parried in my normal voice again. "Jaguar is going to double and you can be a part of it. Let's get involved with one thousand shares."

Silence. I looked at the clock. I scribbled on the paper. I knew he was testing my patience. After a full minute he broke in, still as Foghorn Leghorn.

"Is fahve hunderd shayahs good, Sah?"

"What is your social security number?"

"Excellent!" he cheered. "You've got an offbeat way of making the client feel comfortable, even if you're not your typical blue-collar type salesman. You may find that the guy in auto-body is not your best niche, so it's important to figure out who's going to like you in general and zero in on that group."

I was beaming and instantly popular. Everyone wanted to role-play pitches with me. Dick went from person to person practicing for the rest of the week. The repertoire of strange voices and accents we came up with was great fun-- Hermes' kind of fun.

The last day of sales training we were back in our seats, hopeful and exuberant.

"Ok, I'm going to be brief and let you out-of-towners have the day to explore the city," he announced at noon, looking at his watch. "A few things…"

"First, don't ignore the secretary. You want the guard dog to lick your hand, so take notes on anything personal she gives you. If she has a baby, ask how it's doing, write down its name, put that in your notes. Otherwise call when she's out, because she's there to protect the business owner and I guarantee you he's putting in long hours—like you'll be doing."

"Second, ask for referrals. When you sell someone a stock, immediately ask who else he knows who's in a position to take advantage of a winning situation. A referral is a warm call not a cold call so you already have one foot in the door. If the stock goes up a couple of points, call him back for another referral. Warm calls are the easy way to grow your business."

"Third, lists. The key is to get through the list quickly. Work directly off the list and never copy it. Remember you have five seconds to make your stand."

"Annual reports are a good source of leads. So are newspaper announcements of promotions and even deaths, although all of this works better in the rest of the country than it does here in the City. Get to know professionals in non-competing businesses like lawyers, doctors, dentists, and accountants. Treat them right and they'll send along their accounts. If your clients need a lawyer or an accountant, give him a referral and stay friendly. This way everybody wins."

"Remember, enthusiasm sells. Keep yours up by staying on top of the quarterly reports and the press releases for your stocks. Try to visit the corporate headquarters and meet the people involved. Sell the same stocks to everyone and really stay on top of them instead of owning a hundred different stocks. Building a big position sets you up for a big payday down the road, when you will have a new idea ready to roll that money into so you can keep on surfing."

"Now one last thing," he said, folding his arms. "I don't want you to treat each other as personal friends. I want you to treat each other as friendly competitors who inspire each other. If someone's hot and opening accounts ask him or her what's up—or better yet, go sit by his desk and listen and learn."

"Copy what works. There's room for everyone in this business if you're not looking for management, unlike most professions where there's a pyramid to climb. So get close to whoever's doing well and hang around him until some of it sticks to you, too. Success breeds success. And you guys who succeed quickly, share your ideas freely. There's plenty of stock to go around. You don't have to do anything else because salespeople are natural imitators."

He slapped his hands together.

"Now go out and enjoy the City."

We applauded. With a courtly bow holding one hand in front and another behind, he left the stage. I saw a limousine out on the street waiting. I was in awe. I had met Another Hermes, a double of the god.

....

Wolf showed me to my desk, which was opposite Mal's and next to Messero's in the vast empty room. The only thing on it was a phone, a computer screen, and a Reverse Telephone Directory.

"Did Dick do the striptease?" Wolf asked me.

I nodded.

"Did you like it?"

I didn't answer.

"Go ahead," he said, relenting, "make a business for your self and try not to bother me."

I started dialing my first list, but Mal kept trying to catch my glance. She wanted to talk after every single call.

"I'm calling you Fester from now on," I told her suddenly.

"Like the bald fiend from 'The Addams Family'?"

"Fester!"

"Fine with me," she said, and soon the whole office was calling her Fester, which pleased me to no end.

Fester seemed to like her new popularity, but these pleasantries were only momentary diversions. I kept my face in the cheese grater, grinding away at my normal sense of self. It was Hermes calling, not me.

"I'm calling you with an investment that *nobody doesn't like*," I said, singing the famous jingle to people who wished they hadn't answered the phone. "It's Sara Lee."

Fester copied my pitch, but she kept looking at me imploringly after every call. We were in a race and she was tossing golden apples across my path.

Her face went long with the constant rejection. The next week, she brought in a small mirror that she clipped to her cubicle wall at eye level so she could watch herself making calls.

"If I'm not smiling the sale won't happen," she explained, fixing a Gorgon smile on her face for hours at a time.

"Please open an account with me," I heard her pleading to a stranger on the phone at the end of the day. "I can't go home until I open an account today and I've got a JAP daughter who needs a new ski outfit."

My goal was to get through the *no's* as quickly as possible to reach the ultimate *yes.* Once I sensed a dead end—usually a lack of funds--I got off the phone without letting the *no* people even finish their sentences. I was under no obligation to listen to their song and dance to Nowhere, and I took none of it personally, because it was Hermes they were interacting with, not me.

After the first few thousand calls, it became a kind of parallel life. When I got home at night I would thank the picture of Hermes and tell him, 'Good job today' or 'That was for you, Hermes.'

I stuck with the blue chips.

"I don't need a broker from E.F. Hutton to tell me to buy GE," said Mr. Jones.

"But you do need one to get you to actually do it."

Selling is the quintessential business act and people have been doing it since the beginning of time. Hermes is in our genes like all the gods.

Dialing for hours every day and three nights a week, a warm, monotonous rhythm replaced the stark loneliness of cold calling. We all cold-called together and we all suffered together. I was exuberant on the phone with people who didn't know me and who knew I was after their money, people who had been cold-called a hundred times before and who probably had more investing experience than me. I kept dialing for the chance of being likeable and convincing enough for someone to give me a shot.

I told Big Nose that Fester was driving me crazy.

"Her inability to shut up is going to sink her," he said grimly. "Just don't let her drag you down with her."

She wouldn't stop trying to get my attention so I started facing sideways towards the windows, insisting that I liked the view.

Big Nose was calling new investors.

"I've got a list of plumbers and electricians. These guys have a hundred, two hundred grand stashed under the mattress and no one's calling them because they don't live in the right neighborhood. But they own their home clear and save every penny they make."

"I bet they like your accent, too," I added, "and your blue-collar vibe."

My voice on the other hand suited women, according to Big Nose.

"They like the boyish types," he explained. "And you're not a threat to any woman, so you should call brawds all day."

"I don't need a broker," said Mrs. Jones.

"Mrs. Jones, successful investing requires a minimum of transactions and a maximum of good ideas. GE is a stock you can hold onto for a lifetime."

Women liked that part because it sounded like a marriage vow—Hera's fantasy of a Zeus who stays true to her forever.

"Why should I invest with you?"

"Because of my fabulous personality and good taste," I replied with enough irony to let even the dimmest wit feel the elbow in her ribs. The levity reassured Mrs. Jones with its familiarity. A friend in a reputable firm with a hundred years of history would be investing her money safely.

Older folks wanted me to be dead serious. For them, I enunciated every word as though reading a legal document out loud. I learned to modulate my voice to speak as slowly or as quickly as the person I was calling. For Jewish prospects I turned up the Boston accent to add that hint of Ivy.

"Would you like our firm's opinion of the stocks you own?" worked well on people who already had brokers.

I kept dialing for dollars, letting the persona run loose like an athlete.

"And if you hold it for ten years you can watch the quotes from your television by the pool."

One woman yelled at me for bothering her during working hours.

I barked at her a la Three Stooges.

"What are you selling, darling?" came her gentle voice once she caught her breath from laughing.

I got the first fifty into Sara Lee and GE. Then I went hunting for new ideas. The firm researched 100 stocks and left it up to the broker to decide what to buy. The rating system was simple enough, from 1 to 5, but it was important to know what price a stock was when it was given the rating. A 1 at 30 isn't as good as when it was given at 20 six months earlier. Of course, I learned all this the hard way—pity, the poor turtles.

Big Nose was buying Disney and I asked him if he ever went there.

"Sure," he said, "I once nailed this brawd in a Snow White outfit. She had all that pasty makeup on while I fucked her up the ass. I told her to keep shouting in a little cartoon voice, 'fuck me, fuck me', while I slapped her ass telling her to shut the fuck up. It was hot."

He got me selling an investment called DUIT, or Directs Unit Investment Trust, a one-year stock portfolio investment with a built-in commission the client never sees.

"The scumbags love them," said Big Nose. "That's the fun as far as they're concerned: they think they got you workin' for nuttin'."

It was excellent for cold calling.

"Hello, Mr. Jones, I'm calling with a one year stock investment that has averaged twelve percent for the last ten years…"

The conversation usually started with a sigh on the other end of the phone while the guy tried to figure out how to get off the line, so I got the pitch down to three seconds flat.

"Do you have ten thousand dollars for a great idea averaging twelve percent?" I'd ask. I might as well have been asking him his dick size.

It was easy to tell who thought ten thousand was a lot of money and who didn't. I could see through all the lines like

'I'm not investing right now', 'my father takes care of my investments', and 'I don't believe in calling people at home.' That meant there was no money there and I got off the line immediately.

The call back was trickier. Now, the secretary knows who's calling and that her boss doesn't want to be bothered. Half the time when he did take the call he had no idea who the Hell I was even when we talked five days before.

"I sent you the DUIT brochure," I'd tell him.

"I didn't get the information," he'd say or, "I haven't had a chance to look at it," and then I'd say, "No problem, let me sum it up in ten words…"

Big Nose started skipping the first step and telling prospects they had already spoken.

"Did you receive the information I sentcha?"

Most were too polite to deny it.

"That way you don't have to wait for the second call to close," he told me gleefully. "No one reads anything you send anyways. They feel like idiots for not remembering they spoke widja so I tell them about the investment as if it was our second go around. Only one guy caught me in the act because he was outta town at the time."

The reactions of people to the intrusion on their privacy varied from polite annoyance to downright hostility. I tried to make light of it.

"Surprise, surprise, you didn't know you were just about to start a six hour conversation with a total stranger," I tried or, "You will relish the day we met on the phone."

LOL's or Little Old Ladies sometimes liked getting a call from a young man with education but they were a dangerous lot to mess with, because as soon as the investment goes south they turn into innocent victims whose husbands used to manage their investments.

Every evening when I went home, I *gave* my cold calls to Hermes, vowing in front of the altar that it was he who was calling and not me, and that I was doing it for him. "Thank you, Hermes," I told the image, "We'll do it again tomorrow."

My sacrificial offering to the god consisted of one hundred connections a day, no matter how late it got. It was rote work and the only thing magical about it was the resilience to ignore the rejections and see them as happening to some poor sucker with his face stuck in a cheese grater.

"You'll get the rest of their money in five years if you treat them right," Wolf assured me, pleased to be signing new account forms almost every day. I suspected he was counting on inheriting them.

The golden moment was the one call close. That was like finding a *hermaion,* a 'gift of Hermes', like a twenty-dollar bill on the sidewalk. Hermes really likes you when you can introduce yourself to a total stranger on the phone and by the time you hang up, he's sending you a check.

Most accounts took three calls and one guy took twenty calls before he finally bought a hundred shares. I took it as a personal victory until I realized that he would always take twenty calls to convince him to move on a stock. Only Herakles the Hero has something to prove: Hermes wants the easy way out.

Whenever it got really nasty, I apologized quickly and hung up before Mr. Jones could finish his tirade. Our lines weren't traceable in that era so I liked to leave the guy venting into a dead receiver like Odysseus taunting the Cyclops.

One time a guy looked up the firm and asked for me by name just to yell at me for hanging up on him. From then on I repeated my name incorrectly as I ended a bad call.

"This is Mike Mahoney signing off," I'd say while he raged, trying to scramble his brains.

One guy was friendly enough and eager to talk but every time I tried to close he would tell me to call him later. I gave him three stocks in a row that went up and still he wouldn't open an account.

"He's calling his discount broker with your ideas," said Big Nose, "Give him TWA and see what happens."

"TWA is going belly up," I protested.

"That's the joke."

Now I was venturing into Autolycus, Hermes' criminal son.

"It's a turnaround story," I told the prospect, snickering about 'turning around' behind the receiver. "There are whispers about a takeover and the Feds coming in to resolve the dispute with the union."

"Let me think about it," he said, "Call me back next week."

"I've told you everything you need to know," I said, setting the trap. "I want you in this in a big way with serious money. I don't often feel this strongly and I've given you three stocks in a row that went up. You don't want to miss this opportunity, Mr. Jones. I really have to insist."

"You really like this stock?" he asked, teasing.

"It's hot and you have to act quickly if you want the full effect," I promised him. "It's not going to stay at 4 for very long. I'm trying to make a change in your quality of life." Autolycus was speaking his doubletalk as Big Nose stood over me with thumbs up.

"You're a broker so your job is to make him broker," he laughed when I hung up.

Three days later the man called me enraged. The stock was fifty cents.

"You gave me that piece of shit!" he screamed into the phone.

"What do you mean, sir?" I asked in an overly polite tone, "I sold out the day after we spoke when I got new information. But it doesn't matter because we didn't buy it after all. I would've called you at 3 and gotten you out."

"You said to buy it!" he screamed.

"But we didn't," I answered, "In fact, you still don't even have an account here." I gave Big Nose a high five as he listened on the speaker. "And how many shares would you have bought if we'd gone ahead with it?"

"Ten thousand fucking shares," he moaned.

"Would you like to hear my latest blue chip idea?" I asked him, playing the Vienna Choirboy.

He hung up.

Hermes is an amoral god. He is friendly and helpful but he's used to the ups and downs of life and doesn't really care so long as the bad stuff happens to someone else. In Hermes' world, everyone is on the take and politeness is a game.

But he gave me a filthy mouth. Every sentence was studded with *fuck* and *shit*--and everyone else spoke that way downtown. Big Nose greeted me every morning with *fuck you* delivered with comic hostility. This was Hermes of the Underworld, the friend of Hekate, the Witch who runs with dogs and sniffs the dog shit side of life.

As soon as I got off the train in the Village the swearing stopped and my language became civil again, so the spell was tied to the location, the same magic that makes even nuns swear like troopers once they get behind the wheel of a car.

The witch sees everything and she doesn't judge. When Persephone is raped, Hekate says nothing, because she expects nothing less than disaster and shit in life.

Into the Labyrinth

One morning when I came in everything was different. There were thirty new brokers in the room and no more empty desks. Coffin was packing up his things and moving into one of the side offices.

Wolf came by and told us that Coffin was stepping down from management instead of retiring "due to health concerns." The firm had raided a Merrill Lynch office and brought all the brokers onboard including the manager, Paul Gluck, who was moving into the paneled office.

Wolf's eyes were red and swollen. I surmised he was passed over for management and that Coffin was going to stay on as a broker instead of retiring altogether.

Gluck was a short, bald man in a beautiful Italian suit. He shook our hands and told us younger brokers to join him in the conference room for lunch.

When the bagels and sandwiches arrived we gathered around the large mahogany table as the older brokers milled around the glass walls, peering at the lunchtime offerings.

On the other side of the glass was a dark-haired Italian looking woman, elegantly dressed in red, giving us a sympathetic and curious stare. She was more striking than beautiful, with a large nose and dark almond eyes. She was heavy around the hips with a thin trunk that sat on top like a vase on a table.

Gluck wasted no time getting down to brass tacks.

"As you can see, there are nine of you and no more desks. Unfortunately, I have several people coming in who need them, so we're down to four seats. You do the math. Maybe it's time to ask yourself if you'd be happier working for the telephone company, sitting behind a desk pushing paper or spending the day high up on a pole in the fresh air, connecting red to red and black to black with no need to wonder if the scumbag is sending in a check or not. Seriously, I've got connections there and I can forward any one of your resumes tonight if you'll help me out because as you can see, I'm in a conundrum here."

He looked around with sarcastic sympathy.

"I can't emphasize enough that being a broker is not a job or a position. It's a business. It's your franchise. We just give you the phone and some questionable research. So if you'd like a guaranteed retirement then do me a big favor and give me your resume so I can call my friend at the phone company. Any takers? Please?"

He glowered at us like a lieutenant at boot camp. We all looked down except for Big Nose, who returned his gaze defiantly. My stomach rumbled ominously.

"Now each of these desks costs me forty thousand dollars a year when you count the phone, the insurance, the secretary, everything," he continued. "You all know your numbers and I know them, too. Mahana here has been doing eight thousand a month and Big Nose is doing nine, so obviously the clients have no idea what he looks like."

At this we guffawed but our laughter could not conceal our terror. It seemed natural that the short man in charge would pick on the tallest one of us.

"I'm going to meet with each you for ten minutes and we'll arrive at a decision together that I'm going to make."

We smiled back in terror like submissive monkeys.

I reached for a bagel and started dressing it with lox and cream cheese.

"Yes," Gluck said cheerfully, "eat up boys." With that he helped himself to the lunch spread.

At that moment, the striking dark woman tapped on the glass.

"Can I take some lunch, Paul?" she asked. Her voice was low and as smooth as water. Behind her stood a bald, red-faced fat man who was so anxious to get at the food that he started pushing her into the room. She turned around and looked at him but said nothing.

"Becker, mind your manners," Gluck barked. "There's plenty of lunch for everybody as long as you get served last. Mahana and Big Nose—you go eat at your desks. Yes, you two have desks. And your buddy Wolf is taking seat number three so there's really only one desk open, my friends. I need the rest of them empty by this afternoon."

"The chosen two," said Fester, nodding curtly as she painted a bagel with cream cheese. The others looked at us with envy as I took my bagel over to my desk with Big Nose to avoid making eye contact.

"Look at it this way," I whispered, "We're beating the odds already."

"He can be awful but he isn't always like that."

It was that beautiful, melodic voice tripping over my shoulder like water splashing off a rock. I turned around to see the dark Siren in the red dress smiling at us.

"I'm Jill," she said, holding out her hand.

We shook hands.

"He can be so mean and he wonders why people hate him."

Hers was not a conventional beauty, but she made the most of her gifts. She wore silver hoop earrings and bold mascara that made her eyes look like dark windows in the shadows. Her velvet red dress was voluptuously tailored to highlight her virtues with a plunging but discreet cleavage. Her comportment was erect and graceful. I asked if she studied dance.

"How wonderful of you!" she exclaimed, flattered. "Yes, I did use to dance. Are you a balletomane?"

"I am going to buy season's tickets to everything as soon as I have an income that matches my good taste," I answered with a droll smile.

She wore a large ring with a giant red garnet that glinted with a low fire.

"I hate that he makes things so tense around here," she said, shaking her head and her hoop earrings. "There's no need to. We need all the emotional support we can get."

I warmed up to the Earth Mother she was offering.

"Did you dance professionally?"

"I was in performances but I never got paid, so I guess that means 'no'."

I hesitated, assessing her figure, and she saw me looking.

"That was ages ago," she smirked, slapping my wrist flirtatiously. "I came here to get a real job as my father called it. It was very hard to give up dancing until he cut me off. What can I say? You can't dance if there's nothing to eat and I couldn't bear living at home."

"Reality can get in the way of dreams," I said, "just as Zeus hems in Dionysus."

"So you're a philosopher," she marveled. "Somehow dancers seem to make it on a wing and a prayer. They're never rich unless they marry well. I didn't stick with it as long as I could've but it's a short life. I could have had five more years and that is one my great regrets."

We looked at each other and I began to feel a little uncomfortable.

"And what about you?"

"I'm a would-be intellectual who also realized the importance of food. I've written some poems."

"How delightful," she said, thrilled. "I dated a poet once but it didn't work out. He was gay and only pretending to be straight for his family's money."

She looked around the room and announced, "There's someone with culture in the office!" No one looked up from his desk.

"You mustn't underestimate people," I told her. "Maybe Gluck goes to the ballet."

At this she scoffed.

"Don't get me wrong, he's not all bad," she said. "In fact, he's something of a father to me." She seemed to be choosing her words carefully.

Meanwhile, the other young Turks filed out of Gluck's office with long faces. They had one hour to pack their desks. I avoided their faces. Fester went in last and when she came out she sat at her desk again.

"Welcome to the survivors club," said Big Nose. So it was all decided beforehand, and she was chosen out of deference to Coffin, her father-in-law.

I saw Jill in Gluck's office looking through a stack of account sheets.

"How's your girlfriend?" asked Big Nose. "I see she's in there getting their accounts. I bet Wolf gets the rest as a booby prize for missing out on management."

"She's charming."

"She sleeps with the guy," he said, "and he gives her all the call-in's. Every time someone uses the 800-number it goes straight to her desk. She's like a grizzly bear waiting for the salmon to pass by to scoop them up."

"How do you know all this?" I asked.

"I'm friends with the receptionist, Louise, who does the 800-number."

"You mean you're banging her."

He made a face as if to say, 'obviously'.

"That Jill is a killer like the rest of them," he warned me. "Don't go falling for her sentiment. No one is nice around here."

I floated over to Jill's desk as the office emptied out and the sun was setting behind the *Ficus* in front of her window. She was sorting through the stack of papers Gluck gave her.

"Oh Michael," she cried, "don't come in right now."

She picked up an aerosol can and frantically sprayed the room and I smelled floral air freshener—and something else.

"I've got a terrible stomach," she explained with an embarrassed smile.

"It might be the mozzarella and peppers you're slicing up there," I observed. She had quite an elaborate snack laid out on the desk next to the account sheets.

"Would you like some?"

"Not unless you want me to clear your sinuses for good," I answered, pleased to be familiar. I had a Hermes sense that she could be a convenient ally.

"You've got a bad stomach too?"

The fresh scent of flowers enveloped us in smothering sweetness, blotting out the rest.

"I was wondering if you could do a little dance around the room," I said. "Just show me a few steps. Everyone's gone."

"Are you serious?" she asked and then leaned in to look at me. "You're serious."

She walked around the room in preparation with her arms out beautifully and her shoulders down. This little promenade transformed her as if the god was taking possession right before my eyes. She dashed off a few graceful moves and ended in an easy attitude. I clapped at this vision of Artemis the Graceful.

"How about a pas de chat?"

Once again, she became animated as she swept around the office with her arms out, letting her dress billow in a lovely breeze of movement, throwing in a series of pas de chats and finishing in a graceful lunge.

I cheered. I rejoiced to have this one oasis of Apollo's ideals in this desert of money and numbers.

We formed a provisional friendship like travelers sharing the road for a stretch. There was no mention of socializing outside the office and no sexual tension. She seemed to know I was gay and we avoided the subject politely. I stopped by her office a couple of times a day, sometimes bringing apples or strawberries from the fruit stand down on the corner. Always the conversation revolved around the latest ballet reviews, which I began reading in the paper assiduously.

I couldn't care less if she was sleeping with the boss. Ours was a friendship of convenience—a Hermes friendship— and he is an amoral god. Hermes never judges, he only estimates. I liked Jill talking to me like a confidante, even if we could never really trust each other. Everyone downtown is a cannibal.

....

Becker, the red-faced fat man, sat in the corner office behind us. His son, Ephraim, who was as thin as a rail, sat next to him wearing the traditional garb of the Hasidim with sideburns and tassels.

I could hear Becker breathing heavily from twenty feet away. There was a parade of Hasidim through that room, a strange sight in a modern office.

"Hasidim," said Big Nose, "but Ha don't believe 'em."

"The Smith Brothers have arrived," he announced as a trio of visitors in full regalia came to visit. Fester looked up.

"Nuns are funny looking, too," I noted, watching Fester carefully.

"They'd be better off getting in some cardio than praying for the destruction of their enemies," said Big Nose.

"No," she said, "they 're praying for their stocks to go up."

One afternoon, four big guys in black suits and two cops showed up. Zeus' goons had arrived to enforce the law.

"Moish, I'll call you right back," said Becker, huffing and puffing. "Things are happening here."

They arrested him in his office and cuffed his hands behind his back.

"Paul," he cried as they led him out. "You have to do something."

"All right everybody, " said Gluck when they disappeared, "Show's over. Get back on the phones."

Big Nose called me when he got the goods from the receptionist.

"It's money laundering. You remember Crazy Eddie, 'his prices are insane'? That's the guy."

The arrest was a short paragraph buried in the Journal the next day. The room was dark and empty but the phone kept ringing, so I started to take the calls. Gluck told me to tell people that the Beckers were sick.

"How can they both be sick?" asked the client, fuming. "This is a business. I want to place an order."

"I'm afraid I can't do that."

"Aren't you a broker?"

"It's after four."

"A market order for tomorrow morning."

I wrote the ticket.

The next morning when I got in the lights were still out in that office but I could see Ephraim's black silhouette at his desk outlined against the sky. He must have come in during the middle of the night.

My phone rang.

"Come in here for a moment."

I walked in gingerly. He handed me a few tickets.

"Please put these in for me."

I knew he was barred from the business but I also knew that favors asked on the Street were not easily declined and never forgotten, for Hermes has a long memory and this was a million dollar producer. I could see the nets falling around me.

The order clerk raised her eyebrows when I handed her the tickets.

"Were you the one who put in the ticket for the opening?"

"Yes."

She made a little chirp but said nothing. No one liked Becker but everyone liked his son, who was only twenty-two and had a wife and three kids and that demanding religion to serve.

He called me back into his office.

"I'm trading to support my father's business," he said. "Gluck bolted at the first whiff of the law. All this after ten years of producing for him."

"That's friendship in the business world," I smirked, peering around to see if the boss saw me in the dark office.

"Do me a favor," he said, handing me another set of tickets.

I saw on the commission run the next morning that Ephraim had done twenty thousand dollars worth of business that day, twice what I was doing in a month. He was back in the office every morning after that, talking softly on the phone with the lights out, and every time Gluck walked by he held his hand over his face to avert his eyes.

My phone rang.

"Do me a favor."

And so I became the messenger of the tickets, another kind of Hermes, helping the thief put his orders at the desk. The daily commission run attested to a brisk business.

I ran into Gluck as I walked out of the dark office and he looked down. He called a meeting a few minutes later and the thirty of us brokers stood in his office.

"I know you're all buzzing about Becker. Let me tell you one thing and I'm going to be crystal clear about this: cover your ass. Because if I am ever informed that you are doing anything off the books, anything that's not one hundred percent kosher, then it's kaddish in the Rockies. Big Nose, do you know what kaddish in the Rockies means?"

"A small house in the mountains?"

"It means big problemo," said Gluck, "or however you say it in Guinea. It means you're on your own. Don't expect me to be your partner in crime. And if we do go to arbitration, don't forget to bring your checkbook."

"Rule Number One: do not accept cash. Rule Number Two: do not say you have inside information. If you do know something, let the enthusiasm in your voice convey it, but say nothing. So if you know something, come see me and I'll help you work on the pitch, but you never told me anything either. I just happened to like the stock on my own the same day you talked to me."

"Okay, Big Nose, what are you pitching?"

He looked up, his big face startled.

"Ugly idea," said Gluck, and we laughed as men do around the power of Zeus.

"C'mon, I see the commission run, you're doing something."

"Wang."

"I'm not asking about your personal life."

"WANB. I've got thirty clients in it, a total of twenty thousand shares."

"That's a beginning," said Gluck, "Thirty clients and twenty thousand shares is a very good start. Give me your pitch."

"Da old guy Wang is dying and will probably sell the company so his sons can get the cash."

"And that's the pitch?"

"Let's staht with one hundred shares."

"At least you're closing," said Gluck sarcastically. "Hey, if you do nothing else, at least close. But tell me more reasons to buy the stock."

"The guy's kids aren't that bright, so he knows he has to sell. One of the son's in rehab. It happens all the time. The first generation is bright and works hahd and the second one blows the money."

"And which generation are you?"

"May I have your social security number, please?"

"What were their sales last quarter?" snapped Tucker.

"121 million, up 12% over last quarter and 22 % year over year."

"How's their cash flow?"

"Three times debt flow."

"I thought you were holding out on us. You see, you can't only have the sizzle, you need the steak, too. Big Nose has done a fine job of learning the facts and formulating a pitch that matches his own, unique, half-witted style. And he tried to close on me twice. That's what I want: a room full of closers."

He walked around the group and laid his hands on the shoulders of a very slim young man with thin, cold lips and an aquiline face.

"This here is Phil Way. He's someone you all can learn from. He joining us from Lehman and he brings that particular work ethic with him. The guy cold calls in his sleep. I want you to watch him and listen and be just like him."

The slim man rolled his eyes.

"I need a few more Phil Ways. The Lehman boys have a certain blood thirst that I want you all to catch. He's a money warrior who works non-stop and long hours, and it's paying off big time for him. Right, Way? It got you that place in East Hampton."

Phil nodded in agreement.

This was Apollo the Wolf again, the god that makes a man desire the green pastures of another man. He is a merciless god. I thought about Jim, who also worked hard but who didn't do so at the expense of others. His Hermes was tempered by Apollo's respect for the law and for justice—then again, he wasn't in the sales end of the business.

"Way's got a fourteen percent return on assets," he marveled. "Now that is something to aim for. Then you can send your kids to school, buy that summer place, drive a decent car, get your wife or girlfriend that mink and finally get that second blowjob."

The room roared.

I caught Big Nose on the way out of the meeting.

"Fourteen percent is amazing," I said. "That's twice the market average."

"Fourteen percent on assets, moron, not return on investment," he snickered. "That means he eats up fourteen percent of their money every year in commissions. He's a shark. He has to cold call because he strips them bare and they leave him once they realize the house is on fire."

He called me later with more info, because Big Nose was the kind of guy everyone confided in.

"Our friend Phil Way is banned from cold-calling in five states, including Florida where he ate his way through a number of retirees. When a guy as smooth as Way calls Main Street from Wall Street, they fall under the spell."

I cared about my clients. I wanted to be Apollo the Keeper of Flocks, who watches out for their wealth, or Hermes the Shepherd, minding the herd.

The sheep have to trust you if you want them to follow you, and the quickest way to earn an investor's trust is to talk him out of buying something. Then you can pounce a week later with another stock because you know he's itching to invest. But if there is no money behind that, "it's time to lock in the profits, Mr. Jones," and then stick him in a mutual fund because there are bigger fish to fry.

....

The legendary rally of the Eighties kept fueling the collective hard-on. Everyone was feeling rich and conspicuous consumption was the order of the day. The perennial bull market spawned new confidence and a shameless flaunting of wealth as the economic Icarus flew higher and higher towards his dizzying fate.

My workouts became manic as the spots spread on my tongue and a lymph node on the right side of my neck grew as big as a nickel. Was it always that large? I had never noticed it sticking out like that and I saw the barber staring at it nervously in the mirror.

A couple of purple marks appeared on my calf. I seemed to recall banging my leg against a bar at the gym. When the bruises didn't go away, I scratched at them with my fingernails and then with a butter knife until they bled. When they healed the marks were still there, so I kept scraping them.

I wondered about the flu I had a year ago, and how wild I was when I first gave myself to Eros in the Big City. My head was in a fog but I was busy working.

The market was bubbling with what the Fed chief called 'irrational exuberance'.

"It can't go on like this," predicted Big Nose. "The market's been too good for too long. I got a stock tip from a shoeshine the other day, and that can't be a good sign."

"Why not?" I asked, my Athenian spirit offended.

"You need someone to sell to," he said gravely.

Everyone spoke about the Market as if it was a person. Analysts pored over data trying to figure out 'what the Market is telling us' and 'what will it do next' as if it had a mind of its own. Fortuna was our Muse and she did whatever she wanted and usually what wasn't expected.

The raging bull made me horny. Eros and Hermes led me out at night looking for action. My legs soon had a dozen sores where I had scraped the purple bruises off, so I limited myself to blowjobs at the bathhouses and dirty bookstores with booths in the back.

In the dark I'd go from one booth to the next, closing the door behind me as soon as I found someone ready to get on his knees. Standing there with a smile on my face and my penis sticking through my jeans, I was Hermes of the Crossroads, a pillar carved with only a smile and an erection.

In the world of Hermes, a blowjob isn't sex; it's only heightened conversation. Older guys were especially eager to give me their phone numbers. My obsessive visits to the gym had paid off in a muscular body like Ares that took little persuasion to serve.

Sex for Hermes is about scoring and racking up points, and a blowjob is money in the bank. No man will every say the words, "no thanks, I don't want a blowjob tonight."

When a man dies, St. Peter announces to the world of angels and spirits the number of hours each man spent in his lifetime getting blowjobs. I was banking on making all the straight guys' jaws drop. They seemed to have no idea that reciprocation is an option and that they could have spent the time kicking back and watching sports or porn.

If it felt a little empty, there was freedom in that empty space. I knew how tenuous it was, but married couples can't all be jumping into bed with their spouses out of Hera's obligation; Aphrodite's pure desire is more powerful than her morality.

The bookstores and bathhouses were the ancient crossroads of Hermes. There I was a commodity among commodities, to be traded and passed along. Drugs enhanced the dreamlike world where bodies peer into tiny rooms and exaggerated body parts float around like images of longing. Walking around and around the maze turned me into one of the wandering souls in Tartarus seeking a blood offering that could yield a momentary taste of life. Some encounters were divine, and it was as though I had slept with the god described in Cavafy's poems who slips down from Olympus to indulge his nighttime cravings, or that I had been that god for a few precious hours.

Dusty was always curled up on my pillow when I came home, my little Hestia and the hearth of my home. He stood up and moved aside the moment I walked into the room and waited for me to settle into the blankets before curling up and leaning against my shoulder, purring loudly. I was my Home Self with him and always returned after Hermes had his fill of adventure in the world.

Apollo had gone into hiding. I didn't have time for poetry or for longing. I wasn't looking for The One anymore because plenty of Others will do in a pinch.

Hermes made me see people as interchangeable outlets to pleasure—which sounds heartless until you include friendship in that equation. One blowjob is as good as another unless you can add some friendship and hang around afterwards. Then it's a true delight, and saves a lot of time looking. I kept very busy stacking up my sexual horde for that great day before St. Peter.

....

"You are not analysts," Gluck exhorted us in the weekly sales meeting.

"Analysts sit in their ivory towers at the Financial Center and decide which stocks to maroon us in next. Your job is to stay on the phone."

Whenever he spoke, Gluck transformed from a short, thick, bristly man into a wizard of enchantment. The spell of his fiery speech and reassuring tone made it easy to fall asleep under his incantation. He was a friend of Hermes and his father, Zeus.

"Don't just stare at your belly button and bemoan your fate," he said. "Choppy markets take extra work. Keep in touch with your book. Don't let them worry because when they worry they look for someone to worry for them."

"Success," he said, looking down with a perfect rendering of modesty and reflection, "is the reward for wanting something one hundred and fifty percent. Success happens when you dare to let yourself feel the pain of wanting something so badly you can taste it."

"Throw the safety nets to the wind. Jump right off the cliff, right off that sheer precipice to the bottomless pit of uncertainty where you look among the rocks and crags and in your terror you see a bloodied body way down there below; you're not even sure if it's human, it's so big and misshapen, all bruises and defects and smeared with mud and pebbles, its hair all tangled with filth and you think, Jesus Christ, maybe it's someone you know. You look harder and you think you know whom you're looking at and it's… you see… Big Nose!"

As he shouted his punch line he pointed both arms straight at Messero, who took it all in stride as we roared in laughter that was part humor and part relief that the angry Zeus episode was over.

"So take a stand and get back to work and give me some production," he summarized, "Dismissed."

....

On my desk was a note from Becker. 'See me.'

I could hardly miss him. His huge body wafted into the dark office that morning and moored by skinny Ephraim. From behind the *Ficus* I could hear him gasping and choking like some horrible sea creature gulping down an unwary traveler. He had cost Hutton a fortune in legal fees but the lawyers had kicked the charges and he was back peddling an Israeli perfume stock a friend owned.

I turned around.

"Come talk to me," he wheezed. He must have weighed three hundred and fifty pounds on a small frame. Always sweating heavily, he smelled strangely sweet like oranges. It must have been that perfume. His lips were swollen and red like a butcher's.

"Michael, I want to get you involved in my business."

Jill was walking by and heard this and pretended not to hear, but she listened carefully by the door pretending to examine a document in her hands and looking fretfully at her watch.

"In thanks for your help during my time away," he said, side-stepping the word 'jail', "I'd like to give you some accounts to work on a fifty-fifty basis. These are people I simply don't have time to develop. I've got too many accounts as it is."

When I told Big Nose he sniffed at it.

"I don't trust him."

Sure enough, every one of them had some problem to straighten out, whether a legal issue or a missing dividend or something else awry. Still, I saw the potential in that small pile and was glad to be thrown a bone, even if it had already been chewed on.

"Try this lady. She's very nice," he said, handing me a sheet and barely concealing his glee.

I called Edith Stevens that afternoon. She had a hundred thousand dollar CD in her accounts and sounded like she was a thousand years old. Senility had been making inroads into her reasoning.

"She's crazy," laughed Becker, gloating that he had stuck me with a problem. "A lunatic!"

"Do you ever buy stocks, Mrs. Stevens?" I asked in my Apollo choirboy voice.

"What stocks?"

"The rumor is Jaguar is going to be bought out by Ford."

"How much are they?"

"Jaguar is seven and Ford is forty."

"So Jaguar will go to forty," she reasoned.

"It doesn't work that way."

"Of course that's how it works," she insisted. "One is only seven and the other one is forty. The big one makes the little one go up."

"It's an interesting situation, don't you think?" I asked diplomatically.

"Or else you multiple seven times forty," she said, pausing. "No, that's too much. I know Jaguars are more expensive than Fords, but that's too high."

"That is asking a lot," I agreed with the Mad Hatter. "But don't you think a Jaguar is worth a lot more than a Ford?"

"Oh yes. Buy me ten thousand."

"Ten thousand dollars buys about thirteen hundred shares."

"Ten thousand shares," she replied.

"You are sending me seventy thousand dollars?" I asked, sitting up straight.

"I owned a Jaguar once and it was more than seventy thousand dollars so that's a bargain," she answered. "My late husband, Stanley liked long drives on Sundays. I only take a taxi now. They'll wait as long as you want if you'll tip them."

I made an appointment to meet her after market and pick up the check before I dared to enter an order of that size.

"Four o'clock," she said, delighted, "Come to my little place for tea."

Her 'little place' occupied two floors of an apartment building on Park Avenue crammed with antiques and artwork. An English butler showed me in.

Edith was a tiny woman sitting erect on the edge of a Louis XVI loveseat. She was pale and dapper in a pink pants suit, so it was easy to dispense the compliments.

"Chanel," she explained, bowing as she sat holding her teacup on her knees.

"Tell me about your life," she said, eager for company. "What do you do with your free time, Mr. Michael?"

"Well there's the gym," I began.

"Very good," she said wistfully, "keeping up the body that God gave you. I never did exercise. Women didn't exercise in my day."

"And I write poetry," I added, although I hadn't written anything since I left Academia.

"Poetry!" she cried. "I've got a poet for a broker. How delightful. Then you must think I'm Molly Bloom," she said, looking at my slyly. I deadpanned at the mention of the Joyce character who wanted to 'suck a young poet' and promised to send her a couple of poems. She wrote me a check.

Becker's face twisted when he saw the trade on the commission run.

"Is she lonely, this Edith?"

"She's old enough to be your grandmother," I told him, disgusted.

"How did you get that account?"

"You gave it to me. There was a problem, remember?"

Over the next few weeks, I bought Edith a million dollars' worth of blue chip stocks, steering clear of stocks like Jaguar and going for dividend-paying blue chips for the sake of prudence. She was an L.O.L. with money so I didn't want to take advantage.

"I have a vice president at the bank who knows what we're doing," she informed me, just as I suspected.

"I'd be glad to speak with him."

Becker became obsessed with the million-dollar account he gave away.

"Give me her number."

"She doesn't even know who you are."

"We're partners, remember? I've got an idea for her."
I was obliged to give him the number.

"Don't buy her any crap."

He nodded *no* and laughed.

He bought her thousands of shares of Gruen, an
Israeli perfume company a friend of his owned. He had a
hundred thousand shares in this tiny stock, which was half of
the float, a fact that he thought escaped the traders.

Big Nose advised me to disavow the trade in writing.
I put the note on Gluck's desk. He was sitting red faced with
Becker when I walked into the office.

"Is this a partnership or not?" Becker demanded.

"Give the account back to Becker," Gluck ordered me.

I went into Jill's office and asked her about it.

"The office manager can decide anything about
anyone's accounts," she informed me. "And if you call that

banker you'll get fired," she warned, "so better do what he says."

I retreated.

Meanwhile, Becker joked loudly from his office about becoming a gigolo to an eighty-year old widow.

"Yeah, a jiggle-oh," I called back to him.

He soon told the old lady about *the fagola* who left him the account. I wanted to warn her but my hands were tied.

I had thought of myself as a fiduciary, a servant of Apollo—not the Wolf but the Protector—a follower of that god's trust and honesty. But technically--and this was Hermes' reasoning--she was no longer my client. In the eyes of the law she was out of my purview. That is how Hermes works in his heart of treachery, wandering paths of reason that meander away from difficult situations.

Becker was beside himself.

"They're squeezing the shorts," he shouted in delight as the stock moved up from six to nine in a single day on unusual volume as Edith accumulated her position.

Big Nose called me: "She bought sixty thousand shares on margin. I got it from the order clerk. There's no stock left to borrow out there."

"The traders must be scrambling."

"Wait till they realize it's just his big ass squeezing the shorts."

He called me back a half hour later sounding excited.

"He's dumping his own shares and they're listed as transfer and receive. That means they'll be tied up in the mail for three weeks and now he's coming in and bidding up the stock."

"That's manipulation," I said, finally grasping the situation.

It worked for a week. The panicking shorts bought the shares up to twelve and Becker and Gluck were dancing around the office, on top of the world. It was comical to see the short bald man with the beard looking jubilant with Fatso like Medieval revelers in a painting by Bosch. They thrilled as the traders ran for cover.

Meanwhile, Ephraim remained strangely quiet and sat in the dark at his desk saying nothing. He had a family to protect.

"Don't sell any more today," Becker yelled to Gluck across the room, not caring what we heard or thought.

"How much higher till we sell?"

"I want fourteen," came the answer, "that's my magic number."

"Yeah," I called back at him, "the number of meals in a day."

That week, Gluck hired a stripper for Becker's supposed birthday, but we knew what they were celebrating. She arrived in a business suit for the weekly meeting, holding out a few charts before suddenly stripping down to a G-string and pasties, then dancing lewdly in front of us. Jill stood aghast while Gluck told her to get off her high horse.

The stripper did a lap dance on Becker's knees.

"He looks right at home in the whorehouse," I whispered to Big Nose.

"I got a polaroid for your wife," Big Nose told him.

Jill walked back to her office. I went over to her.

"We should hire a man for one of the girls to make it fair," I offered.

"Don't ever do that to me," she said sternly.

"Was he cute?" I was guessing it had happened once.

"It was humiliating. If only the men in this business weren't such pigs. Do you think anyone here ever asked himself about the meaning of life? Even once?"

I could see tears starting so I went back to fetch her a piece of cake. The stripper was fiddling with her G-string and Gluck told her to stop there. Jill took the cake eagerly and put one hand on my cheek saying, "Don't ever change."

Gruen collapsed the next day when the traders figured out what was going on. It opened at three and shot down to one, and Becker and Gluck were screaming at each other in the corner office with the lights out. Ephraim kept looking down at his desk. When Becker walked by he saw me staring and gave me a look: "What?"

"You could've just bought Pepsi and GE," I said.

"Asshole."

But the fun was just beginning. Edith's banker was on the phone with me as soon as she got the margin call after lunch. I sent him over to Gluck, who came racing out of his office and into Becker's dark office screaming, "You fucked me, you fucked me!"

Becker was defiant. His fat body shook as he stood there sweating through his shirt.

"Ten years I'm a producer for you."

"You've nailed us both on that piece of shit!" Gluck shrieked, this time pushing his fists against the swollen mass of Becker's body.

Becker picked up the account books from Ephraim's desk as his son protested, "Dad don't", and threw them across the room, scattering papers everywhere. The office turned and stared in disbelief as Gluck pushed Becker against the wall, panting.

"You get away from me," blubbered the fat man, drooling.

"You fucking—" Gluck started but then suddenly checked himself, as though someone had pulled him by the hair. Athena's professional persona was back in charge. With his hand still pinning the gasping Becker against the wall, he dropped his shoulders, clenched his teeth, and then walked out of the office, muttering, "You get out now and don't darken my doorway again."

Ephraim had his hands in his mouth as his father wiped his face with a handkerchief he pulled out of his pocket.

Gluck surveyed the room. We were staring at our screens.

"Show's over," he barked.

This time Becker didn't came back. Weeks later, Big Nose told me Becker was peddling jewelry on 43rd Street.

"Is he selling watches out of his coat?"

"His coat could carry a jewelry store and a coffee shop," he said. "Look what I got for three thousand."

He dropped a silk handkerchief in my palm tied around a few stones. Inside the silk I found a half dozen beautiful uncut emeralds.

"See, he's not all bad," he said. "We talked about gemstones as an investment before and he knew I was looking."

Jill came out to admire the stones in my open palm.

"I want this one," she said, smiling and pointing at the biggest one.

"Of course you do, darling."

She admired the stones as my other hand went up to the node on my neck. I bundled up the little treasures and gave them back to Big Nose.

Back at my desk, I pretended to lean on my hand while I continued to feel the large gland on my neck. While I was rubbing the spot, I made eye contact with Jill, who was sitting in her office slicing some mozzarella and red pepper.

"I get tense, too," she said sympathetically. "I wish life was all emeralds and ballet."

I took my hand off my neck and smiled.

"So how's your business?" she asked from her seat. "I hear you selling blue chips all the time. I like that."

I got up to join her in her office but she waved her hands in mock alarm.

"Not just yet!" she shouted, taking out a bottle of Gruen perfume and spraying it in the room. "My tension goes to my stomach, not my neck."

"So that perfume is good for something."

I made a pot of coffee in the mailroom and served her. It was after market hours.

"I built my business while I was separating from my husband," she told me. "I stopped having a life for three years and stayed nights cold calling like you're doing now. It was like going into hibernation. I threw myself into it just like I did with dancing. That's what you have to do for a while, become obsessed until your business takes on a life of its own—which it will," she assured me with a pat on the hand.

"Put some Dionysus into it."

"Yes!" she exclaimed. "Exactly that." She gave me a slice of cheese on pepper.

"How about a pas de chat tonight?" I asked her, reveling in her attention.

"Not when I'm gassy."

"Pas de gaz."

She laughed and shooed me out of her office.

The next day, Gluck summoned all of the brokers into his office. London had rallied in a big way and the futures were soaring. The bull was running on fumes.

"Just a quick meeting," he said, "to test your sports knowledge."

The group smiled in relief.

"Who struck out the most batters in baseball history? No, too easy. Who hit the most home runs in any league? No, too easy," he smiled, his joke set up for the ritual third round. "Who took the most balls on the chin?"

"We give up. Who?"

"Liberace," he cackled.

A groan rose through the room. Liberace was in the hospital dying of AIDS.

"Hey, the poor guy's on his deathbed and I understand that you scumbags are making a pool over when he dies," he said, moral outrage creeping into his voice.

3ilence.

"How much is it up to?"

"Four hundred."

"Put me in for Saturday at four pm," he said. "Dismissed."

Fellow of the Night

I buried myself in Hermes' downtown Underworld where everyone is a voice on the phone and events stream by with arbitrary predictability like price trends on a screen. As I walked through the World Trade Center in the morning the rushing crowd flowed out of the subway like trout swimming up stream. The clang of the subway turnstile rang out the toil in this daily migration as I told myself that this is what the gods wanted from me, not poetry. Winters and summers came and went and I was interred through dinner at the office, diving into the hunt for new assets and new accounts until the office and its fluorescent lights on late nights took on a homey feeling.

I saw the world in terms of dollars and measured all things in terms of cost. I focused on increasing production through sheer force of effort. The world was a series of numbers on the screen and voices on the phone, cajoling, complaining, objecting, and agreeing to move their money from one place to another. Voices welled up on the phone like souls peering up from dreams, at once strange and familiar. I continued conversations with clients for years and learned to talk to total strangers as though we had known each other for a lifetime.

I was possessed by a demon, able to speak only of dollars. Poetry was shoved aside. Friends were a distraction. I dialed as quickly as I could, racing against an invisible competitor, compelled in a rush to open accounts and gather funds. I was creating something tangible--a real business out of thin air, burning through lists looking for buyers willing to agree to a proposition and send me a check--or better still, a stock certificate emblazoned with some goddess holding cables or thunderbolts in the name of some corporation.

My apartment became an abode of Hermes. It was a place to sleep and eat with a trash bucket full of take-out containers. Only my love for Dusty kept the place feeling like home. I would play Hestia the Homemaker every Saturday with a thorough cleaning including changing his box and a trip to the grocery store for the week ahead for both of us.

I kept the altar stocked with apples and strawberries and ate some every evening staring at the various images I had assembled and thanking Hermes for possessing me again that day.

I was young and capable of long hours for the sake of the future. It was like selling a few years of life for the long term good of having means, I told myself as the weeks and months ground by. Both Apollo and Hermes were bound to serve mortal men for seven years, so the work was mythically sanctioned and meaningful.

My sex life was confined to the booth store with the porn and a short list of regulars in the neighborhood with whom I got right down to business. There were no dinner dates or movies but I was loyal to my regulars and saw virtue in dependability rather than variety. Looking for sex was a complete waste of time when there was someone willing to give me a blowjob just for the phone call. And blowjobs were all I did—and only on the receiving end, since oral sex was considered safe, especially if I was the one getting it. Besides, Hermes had me committed to racking up those points for Saint Peter.

I met one guy, Rusty, at the porno movie theater, where he was servicing guys in their seats, and took his number. Every Wednesday at ten I sat in a chair in his apartment on 29th Street watching sports while he worked on me, transforming me into a faceless smile and erection like Hermes of the Crossroads.

"A good old fashioned blow job," he'd say as he swigged out of the bottle of whiskey on the floor by the chair. His head bobbed like a machine as I marveled at the prodigious neck muscles that kept him going for hours. He wore sweats so he became just a head to me, like a coconut sitting in my lap, and the sex was all about "getting my orgasm removed," as he put it, and I did not disagree.

Head is sheer profit, Hermes told me, and the sex felt like I was getting away with something. I would watch the clock and put in the hours just as I did at work while looking forward to that glorious day with St. Peter.

We hung out afterwards, chatting. When I asked half jesting for referrals, he gave me a few numbers—friends of his who were into the same thing and were looking for something regular.

"I hear you suck dick," I'd say over the phone to a complete stranger after he gave me the go-ahead. They thrilled at the brazen come-on. We were satyrs like Pan, the darling of Hermes, the horny devil who is half goat and half human and always has a hard-on. We'd settle on a certain day of the week or every two weeks to make the most economical use of my free time.

Every call sheet I filled out, every dialing I made brought me closer to my goal of financial independence and freedom. I was hungry for new pools of buyers and new leads. So was Big Nose.

"Let's go to Gambler's Anonymous," he proposed. "You sit in a circle. Everyone tells his tale of woe. Then you get up and say you were the same as them until you found religion. Now you only buy conservative mutual funds and zero coupon bonds. Then you give out your card during coffee and cookies."

"They're broke by the time they wind up at Gambler's Anonymous," I objected. "That's the hole in that idea."

I saw notices for a yachting show at the Javits Center that was open to the public, so I went there looking for leads. The booth owners were eager enough to talk about stocks until they realized I wasn't a customer. They were shelling out good money for booths so I left them alone and took the catalogue home so I could call them when the show was over and the meter wasn't running.

That crowd I pitched Brunswick, a sporting goods company that owns Boston Whalers, a classic harbor boat. It was a hit. From a mere three hundred names I opened fifteen accounts, an incredible rate for prospecting. I was a vampire with a new pool of blood victims that no one else seemed to have thought of yet.

A video show followed, where I walked down the aisles in dark sunglasses looking as bored as I could—these were cool cats—but I went home as soon as I found a copy of the catalogue. When I called Andre Dapeese, owner of Home Video Inc., he told me to come by his studio one late Wednesday afternoon. It was in a warehouse on the west side of Chelsea, a lonely area at the time. I met Andre sitting behind his desk, a middle aged man with a decent belly wearing a Hawaiian shirt and shorts. He wore sunglasses in the fluorescent light, a cool cat like the others.

When he saw me he held up a finger and mouthed, 'wait' while he finished a phone call. That's when I got a good look at the woman sitting on the couch across from him. She was wearing a very short skirt and sat with her legs folded carefully. She was beautiful in her make-up and precision cut blond hair with diamond earrings and had a model's slim waist and enormous melons for breasts. Her sunglasses were giant Jackie O's and her face was relaxed and free of tension.

While Andre chatted, I stood up and began wandering around the corner to check out the loft.

"No, no, Michael!" he shouted after me, panicking as he pressed the phone against his shoulder. "We're shooting in there."

"I won't walk in front of the camera," I assured him.

"It's adult video."

I froze in place, turned around and went back by his desk. The woman on the couch smiled behind her large square sunglasses and then resumed her blank stare.

Andre gave me a hundred thousand dollar check to open the account.

"I'm not getting any younger," he told me with a wink, "So please make it grow."

"So you got Da Peese of de action?" asked Big Nose, excited about my incursion into porn. "There's money in smut," he said admiringly, but I didn't tell him about the Javits Center—I didn't want anyone else to know the location of my gold mine.

I went to every show thereafter. A lot of the exhibitors were entrepreneurs with new money and no stockbrokers yet. When the spring Pret-a-Porter show arrived during Fashion Week, I wore my best suit and added a touch of bronzer and went up to the door claiming to be a model. I was turned back.

"This is only open to trade," I was told by a gruff Irish cop.

"But I'm a model."

"A model liar," he answered, looking me up and down, "It's women's fashions, darling."

I had no time to run out and print a bogus business card and the show was ending at three, so I came back at two thirty looking harried with my collar open and tie loosened. Exhibitors were pushing racks of clothing across the plaza, exhausted from walking on the cement pavement in heels for three days.

This time, the guards didn't even look at me. There were too many people clearing out. I buzzed up and down the show aisles, looking for the red catalogue with the yellow lettering that I had seen in people's hands earlier that day.

No luck. I was about to grab one off a table when a leggy model screamed out, "Hey, that's mine!"

I left the Javits Center gloomily and walked back to the avenue to catch a cab. Standing by the curb with my arm out, I noticed one of the red books in the trash can, lodged under a half eaten hero sandwich. In clear view of the traffic and with no discreet option, I reached in and picked up the sandwich, bumping my suit jacket sleeve against an old cup of coffee as I grabbed the red book with the other hand, victorious.

This didn't go unnoticed. One gay guy from the show stood behind me watching, horrified.

"Here," he said, handing me a five.

I thanked him, dropped the sandwich and took the five gratefully. It paid for the cab home.

The fashion list was a perfect fit. The Jews, gays, and woman entrepreneurs loved my gay vibe.

"Hello, Mr. Jones, I'm calling from EF Hutton with a stock that is going to make you rich and me famous."

That was enough pizzazz to disarm a crowd who thought of stockbrokers as bankers.

"I'm talking about Liz Claiborne, who has made many millionaires in your business. I would like to get you involved with five hundred shares right now."

I didn't waste their time with niceties like asking them how they were doing today. Theirs was a frantic business where sizzle matters more than substance. They were *fashionistas*, followers of Aphrodite and superficial by trade.

I hit them with winged feet and a quick humor so they knew I wasn't going to waste their time. I raced through the list, slipping past the initial objection to being cold called with enthusiasm, modulation of voice, brevity, and quick jibes. These people were open to the fast close so I was soon picking their pockets. Theirs was a Hermes business in service to Aphrodite's beauty, subject to whims and crazes, so they were seducible and used to taking chances with strangers. This herd of marketing pros loved jokes and personality and eschewed white bread innocence, so I let my guard down.

"Liz is my competition!" said one.

"What better revenge?"

"Give me a hundred," he whispered, "But don't tell anyone who works here."

"I'm not asking you to buy an outfit, I'm asking you to take a stand."

"Five hundred."

I'd tell the Jewish ones, "Mr. Jones, you know that Liz Claiborne is really Liz Ortenburg and she's starting a men's line called Clayburn. Isn't that WASPY touch clever? A thousand shares will really get you some serious profits."

"Is that her name?" they'd ask with delight.

"We'll get rich together."

"I thought I was getting rich and you were getting famous."

"Oh you'll remember me," I assured them, and I bought ten shares so I could say that I personally owned the stock without lying.

One woman with a Hollywood British accent moaned when I told her I was calling with a stock.

"I'm getting hammered by Liz," she cried before I could mention the stock, which was down twenty percent. "What have you got?"

"Excuse my language, but you bought that piece of shit?"

"I got buried."

"You should sell it and buy the Gap and put your money in a winner instead."

"They do always seem to come out on top."

She bought five hundred shares and transferred her account to me, "away from that idiot who sold you Liz," I told her. I made a note on her file never to mention Liz again.

Another prospect, a Thai man with a last name with ten syllables bought a hundred shares on the first call because he "liked the sound of my voice". We flirted on the phone. I thought he was a woman at first, because his voice was high and his name, Nat, was ambiguous. He giggled when I called him 'ma'am' and corrected me after my pitch.

"I wonder what you look like?" he asked.

"I'm cold calling naked from the desk down."

"Ooh!"

A week went by and he hadn't paid the bill so to save the account from a sell out, I offered to come pick up the check at his showroom and say hello. The showroom was tucked among the clutter of Seventh Avenue.

I felt like Hercules among the nymphs as all the skinny young models of both sexes tittered around me. Nat was barely five feet tall and looked like a fifteen year-old boy, smiling sweetly as he handed me the check.

"I didn't mail it because I wanted to meet you."

"I thought so."

Our flirtation on the phone devolved into dirty talk. He wanted to get together but I kept putting him off, preferring to keep it at a tease and afraid that he'd lose interest in the account once we actually did anything, because I was familiar with Gay Apollo. After a couple of months, he referred me to his accountant.

Ranjit was from Bombay and didn't sound gay. His voice was deeper than Nat's and he laughed when I mentioned his friend.

"He's into whips and chains." n

He gave me twenty thousand dollars of his own money, but that was only the beginning. As an accountant he was one of those non-competitive professionals with a list of clients I could exploit. His referrals would come with built in trust.

I called Ranjit every day to 'check in'. Soon he referred me to a couple of small accounts but I knew there was more behind them and perhaps he was testing me out.

When Thanksgiving rolled around he told me he had no plans so I invited him to join my family outside Providence. On the drive through endless Connecticut he told me about his one-time Japanese girlfriend who had a fantasy of having sex with him and a black guy at the same time.

"Guess I can't help you out there," I told him. We didn't discuss my sexuality but of course there was no deceiving someone so open.

My family liked Ranjit and he clearly enjoyed himself. My father was relieved I hadn't dragged home another gay buddy and I made a big point of mentioning Ranjit's girlfriend. My little nephew thought he was an American Indian and Ranjit played along. He was pretty dark and handsome.

"We're having an Indian for Thanksgiving,' he whooped. "I can't wait to tell my class."

"Tell them I scalp naughty children," said Ranjit, sticking his tongue out and bulging his eyes like a Gorgon.

We laughed over the dinner table.

"That's the face I make at kids in the grocery store when their mother's aren't looking," he confessed. "They're riding in the cart and suddenly start to cry and the mothers have no idea what happened. Meanwhile I'm just innocently shopping."

On the drive home, Ranjit told me how honored he was to have been invited to my family's house.

"It's the highest compliment you can pay someone in India," he informed me.

That was when he sent me his biggest client.

"They're distant cousins from Bombay and fabulously wealthy. Gadia is the one you'll speak with. Jatia is not always around, but he's the one who's really in charge. Their compound in Bombay is on the peninsula, which has the most expensive real estate in the world. They live like sultans. They have at least thirty Rolls Royce's. They just moved to the States from Japan where they lost two million dollars playing commodities. But they're big boys and can afford it. Now they're buying up hotels all over Florida."

"Where did they get all the money or shouldn't I ask? Sounds like they're trying to hide it."

"Don't ask," he said. "It's probably something awful like guns or heroine but I'm just the accountant so I officially don't know anything. I just keep things tidy. The new company name is Greenland America."

"What's that supposed to mean?"

"Precisely," he answered. "Maybe they sell herring for a living. Let me prepare the way first so they expect your call. They don't like to talk to strangers," he said, holding up his hand in caution as I drove.

"I'll do as you say."

"Also, between you and me, get a check up front before you let them go on a spending spree. These guys stiff people all the time."

I called Greenland America a few days later on Ranjit's say-so.

"Do you import cod?" I asked Gadia, who was eager to hear from me. "I hear it's quite beautiful up there with the icebergs."

"Lots of cod and herring," he giggled over the phone in a throaty Indian voice slightly deeper than Ranjit's.

"You don't sound like you're from Greenland."

He burst into contagious, shrieking laughter, cackling so hard that I could tell over the phone that his belly was shaking. It was so catchy I couldn't help joining in but I fell silent the moment he became serious again.

"You have a stock ideas?" he asked in his strange diction.

"Always."

You offer gooda discount? We like Syrian people. I know your name is Syrian Christian. I know Mahanas before from Latakia."

"That's where my grandfather was born," I told him, surprised.

"Good business people, the Syrians. Very smart," he said rolling his *r*'s.

"I'm buying GE right now."

"It is a gooda stock. What price?"

"Sixty-five."

"Sixty-five is a gooda price. You think it go to sixty-eight?"

"Sure, if you give it a little time."

"Buy me ten thousanda stocks."

"Ten thousand shares? Six hundred fifty thousand dollars, correct?"

My heart was racing.

"Daz right," he said, rolling his *r*'s and giggling with delight.

"I need a deposit."

"Good. Come by. But buy the stocks now and then come by. What you need?"

"Ten thousand," I said, hoping that would cover any shortfall if the stock moved a point before I got there.

"Small change," at which he burst out laughing so hard I joined in again, although Athena's judgment wondered what was so funny. Buying that many shares without a check up front is risky but I put in the trade anyway, then jumped on the train to midtown.

Wolf signed the account form. When he saw the size of the ticket he said he'd like to meet the guy sometime and mumbled something about always liking Indian food, but I kept quiet.

I called Gadia 'the Happy Hindu' and soon perfected an imitation of his voice and laughter. "It is a gooda stock. But me ten thousanda stocks," I chanted as my business took off with his huge volume of trades. In the throaty Indian voice I honed, I sang 'Swami, how I love ya, how I love ya', "I'm just a hunka hunka turban love' and 'we gunto rock onto Electric Avenue, and den we take ita higher,' rolling my *r* lavishly at the end. I liked him and it was all in good fun, in the mocking way of Hermes.

After a few winning trades, I was put through to Jatia, the supposed Uncle. His voice was an intimidating deep bass. He was a serious, Zeus-type executive and not given to giggling. I imagined the whole shady operation lined up like nesting Russian dolls: Nat, Ranjit, Gadia, and Jatia, each one to the right bigger than the one to the left and with a progressively deeper voice.

I never asked where the money came from. *Let sleeping dogs lie*, said Hermes, *the money is green*, but I made sure the account sheet had all the necessary legal information and authentic signatures. My commissions doubled overnight, freeing me to leave the other investors alone in order to make the rent. I split my time on the phone between Gadia and cold calling the Javits lists.

One older man from the fashion show called me to sell out his Liz and close the account. He said his company, JC Penney, was moving from New York to Dallas and that he was accepting their offer and moving with them even though he hated leaving the City.

"But Angelo," I said, "We have an 800 number and now we know each other. Who knows whom you'll be dealing with down there. Why don't I come see you before you go? How's the end of the day? When does everyone leave there?"

I guess that last question was a little suspicious because he said, "Huh?"

I smelled blood. Although Angelo was moving, I knew most fashion types would rather die than leave New York for Texas, no matter how big the bonus might be. The directory would be full of forced retirements and lump sums distributions to roll over.

I sat in Angelo's office at the end of the day, enthusing about how he'll be able to buy a giant house and have a yard and a pool instead of a cramped New York apartment, how warm the winters will be and so on. I kept chatting until we were the last people left in the office. As we walked to the elevator I suddenly asked him where the bathroom was and told him he didn't need to wait for me. As I wandered off in the indicated direction, I scouted out an in-house directory on a secretary's desk. It was two inches thick.

When I got back to the elevator, I was surprised to find Angelo waiting. Quickly, I folded my jacket over the book, complaining how warm it was in there and maintaining eye contact so he wouldn't look down and see what I was doing.

"See you later!" I sang as the elevator opened in the lobby, clutching the new list.

This was a different kind of treasure chest, stuffed full of motivated investors. I opened thirty accounts on that list, bringing in another three million in assets in a month. I had to calm nervous pension holders and explain that an IRA is just the title of the account and that it could house cash, gold, stock or CD's, so long as the money isn't taken out. I emphasized how important it was for them to roll over the check quickly before it became a taxable event, which helped get them to move.

"There's no need to sell your J.C. Penney stock," I promised. "I am just here to protect you from taxes." Of course, once the stock was under my aegis, some great idea for what to do with it would soon surface, like diversifying the portfolio to "lower the risk."

The bull run of the summer of '87 defied gravity as Hermes possessed the multitude. We had been levitating for over a year without earnings to back it up.

Now I could buy anything at the grocery store. That was a watershed. Then I bought my first suit from Barney's.

Gluck was in fine form.

"This is the easiest market in the world to make a living in," he told us in the meeting. "If you aren't making money in this kind of environment, you aren't cut out for this business. When times are tough, you'll wish you had taken advantage of these good times. When you're on a roll, you've got to run with it, so I'm ordering pizza three nights a week for those of you who are motivated enough to stay and cold call, and I strongly recommend you do."

When times were tough, we heard the same speech backwards: "You have to work harder and stay longer hours in tough markets." Evidently there was no good time to take a vacation or kick back. There must be a special place in Hades where burnt-out sales people roll stones up hills only to watch them roll down the other side.

"I've got a serious problem," Gluck began the old song again, "There are ten guys a week banging on my door and I'm out of desks. You've got to put in the extra effort and make the extra calls or make room for somebody else."

"I'm not naming names," he ranted, "I've had it with that game. You know who you are. You know when you go home at night and put your head on the pillow whether or not you worked hard that day and gave it your all. Do you say, 'hey that was a great day. I really kicked ass. I squeezed as much out of today as possible.' Do you say that to yourself when your girlfriend's asleep and there's no one around to bullshit?"

"Everyone here gets the commission run every morning so you all know who's performing and who isn't."

"Michael, for instance, has been grossing fifteen thousand a month, pumping out trades like a real broker in the making. Big Nose is right after him, although you'd never know it to look at him."

Messero made a sheepish grin amidst the taunting laughter of men who counted on the big guy for a scapegoat.

"We've got someone new starting tomorrow. Her name is Rose Isaacs. She's taking the only free desk and there's a long line behind her. She's been in the business for only three months and she's already grossing thirty thousand a month at a boutique, so now she wants to take advantage of a big firm with a reputation and parlay that skill with our research and support crew to back her up. She's going to teach all of you tough guys a lesson in making a business. So take notes and be respectful. Dismissed."

"He'd be a nice guy if he was five inches taller," Big Nose muttered.

"What free desk is he talking about?" I asked him. There weren't any I knew of.

"The one he's clearing right now," he said, nodding towards Gluck's office where Fester was sitting on the chair in front of him crying in her hands.

"One more down."

Fester came back to her desk with a cardboard box and quietly started to fill it with her belongings. Her eyes were misty so I stayed on the telephone, the bagel staring up at me on its paper napkin like the eye of a Cyclops.

She got on the phone and made a few whispered calls, her voice cracking like a dying sea monster.

"I'm sorry," I said, when we finally looked each other in the eye.

"I'm all right," she answered defiantly, her face broken. "He's right. He's right."

That afternoon as soon as Fester left Wolf took her book and started calling her accounts.

"She wanted me to have her accounts," he explained when he saw our faces, but we knew the rules of the game.

The next morning, Rose was at Fester's desk when I got in. I was surprised to see she was Indian with the last name Isaacs. She was quite beautiful, but her low cut blouse and short skirt were risqué for a financial office.

"Hello, how are you?" she said, putting down a doughnut to shake my hand. Her eyes were ringed with mascara like a panda and she wore giant golden hoop earrings. A patent-leather belt almost as wide as her mini-skirt made a feeble effort to cover her underwear when she sat down.

"Don't you love this great skirt?" she asked, standing up and showing off her shapely legs, which were bursting out of fishnet stockings.

"I was going to tell you to put one on," said Big Nose.

"Do you mind a little music?" she asked, ignoring him. I told her I did not and she put a radio on her desk and tuned in a country music station. It was too loud but I didn't bother to complain because I knew someone else would soon enough. Hermes prefers letting others do the fighting for him whenever possible. Only three minutes went by before Gluck stuck his face out of his office and shouted at her to "shut that crap off".

"This isn't a construction site here."

"Bunch of stiffs," she said, adjusting her skirt down an inch but not far enough to hide the top of her stockings.

We were back in the rhythm of work when Rose produced an enormous wind up alarm clock that she placed on her desk by the phone.

"I'm setting it for ninety minutes from now," she explained. "I'm going to cold call nonstop until it goes off and then have another cup of coffee."

She dialed non-stop with a penny stock for which she blatantly claimed to have inside information. Big Nose raised his eyebrows. When the alarm sounded, I leaned in to speak to her.

"You have to be careful about saying you have inside information," I warned her, playing Zeus to her Hermes, "people might be recording your calls."

"Fuck you," she said defiantly. "Fuck everybody. I have to get them do something, don't I? I saw the commission run. You're in no position to give me advice, Mister."

My face froze in a smile as I went back to work, figuring that the gods would have their way with her.

"That's what I like," said Big Nose, breaking his silence. "A macho woman. I bet you're tucking, little Rose. C'mon and lift up that skirt and show us whatcha got."

"I'm more of a man than you are, Mr. Big Nose—and I can see why they call you that," she answered angrily. "Where'd you get that face, in a morgue?"

"And you're not bad looking for an Injun girl," he answered. "You're nostrils aren't too snarling, your voice is normal, and you got a nice figure but you really ought to put on some clothes. We'll call you Injun Rose."

Rose picked up the heavy alarm clock and threw it at Big Nose's face. He caught it mid-air and slammed it down on his desk with a terrible crash.

Gluck came running out of his office.

"What the hell is going on out here?"

I hid on the phone as Gluck called them into his office to make peace. Rose emerged looking annoyed and Big Nose made a cynical smile.

"Anyway, Dick-wad," she said, "It's no one's business how I dress, what I say, or what I do. I'll do whatever the fuck I want. I know what boys like and especially fifty year old men with fat, nagging wives."

"So Rose," said Big Nose, "We're all rooting for your suck-sess."

"Don't you wish."

Her phone rang.

"Listen you fucker," she yelled. "The stock is going to eight and you own it at five. So what if it's four today? Bring that fucking check to the fucking office or I'll come over and tear your eyes out."

Her voice softened abruptly and she whispered into the receiver, "Don't you remember last weekend? Don't you want that again?" Tears started as she searched for the most effective emotion to control the man on the other end of the line. "What would your wife think about all this?" she added ominously.

She slammed down the phone. Then she picked it up and called him back, playing the lover's quarrel.

"Look," she said as tenderly, "I'm sorry I yelled at you. I get all flustered when you don't believe me. But I know this will work. You're only down a measly point or so, what's that anyway? I don't know who's doing the selling but it's going up next week. Drop the check off before two o'clock at the office in Daytona, same as last time. Okay? Thanks. Me, too. Look, why don't we buy another five thousand right here so we'll be up by the time it gets back to six?"

She hung up before the customer had a chance to refuse and put in the order, flaunting the ticket in my face.

"I marked it up a half point. That's three thousand in commission so far today. I've trained them all. I tell them what to do and if they don't, I punish them and they like it."

"C'mon, Rose, show us your bawls," said Big Nose eagerly. "I know you got 'em, big heavy bawls."

She followed us with the crowd of brokers into the elevator to go downstairs to get lunch. It was a full crowd and

Rose was the only woman in the elevator. Big Nose suddenly jumped.

"Rose, watch out!" he said. "That's my dick you're holding."

We stood uncomfortably silent, knowing he had trespassed Apollo's legal boundary of sexual harassment.

"I'm sorry. I thought it was your pencil."

The mocking laughter of men filled the elevator.

I couldn't help but admire Rose's fearlessness. She was like Argus, the hundred-eyed monster fighting on all fronts with the weaponry of threats, inside information, and great legs. It seemed inevitable that Hermes would one day lead her to her doom, as he did when he lulled Argus to sleep with conversation and wine and then cut out all his eyes at once.

It could be a reneg or perhaps something more serious if anyone was recording her calls. I decided to sit back and wait for the calamity to take shape because Rose was riding on Fortune's wheel and cracking a whip as no mortal should.

"Gluck tells me you opened twenty accounts last month on some great list from JC Penney," she told me one morning, bringing me a coffee and smiling sweetly. I smiled back thinking about the other faces I had already seen her make.

"They relocated so I took advantage of the situation."

"Great idea. Bank of New York is moving to Richmond. How do we get in there and do it again?"

"I don't know anyone there."

"So let's apply for a job and steal a directory."

"Do you have a resume?"

She reached into her desk drawer and pulled out a resume that was already updated to show her employment at Hutton as of last week.

"They're not hiring," I assured her, "they're probably busy firing people right now or convincing them to move with them."

"They're losing half the staff with the move," she countered. "We'll go at the end of the day like you did. No one will be working late if they're quitting. Morale must be terrible there," she added with mock sympathy.

"How do we get in?"

We walked up to One Wall Street just after five and met the security guards in front of the elevator banks. One tall man approached us.

"May I see your passes, please?"

"Actually," said Rose, holding her resume up for the man to see, "we're here to bring our resumes up to Kathy in personnel before she goes home for the day. I've got an appointment with her tomorrow and wanted her to have this beforehand. You know how hard it is to get a job with your company," she added, "and there are going to be a lot of openings soon."

She looked at her watch and got frantic. "Oh God, it's almost five and I promised her the resume before the end of the day. She's going to think I'm a flake before I even get to meet her. Can't we just run up and drop them off with her secretary?"

"Kathy Simpson or Kathy Karos?" he asked.

"Kathy Simpson."

"She's on ten," he said, "I believe she's left for the day. You can leave them with me and I'll be sure Miss Simpson gets them in the morning."

Rose began to cry.

"I knew it," she sobbed, "I'm not going to go to Richmond now. I promised I'd bring it by their office today."

The man softened. The firm was leaving and he knew the mood was tense.

"Go leave it under the door and run right back down then."

"We promise."

Rose could see my admiring glance as she thanked him, wiping her tears and smiling flirtatiously.

"Are you a double agent?" I asked her in the elevator. She was Hermes the Spy.

"I pulled the name out of a hat."

We got off at ten and saw the main reception desk for Personnel. No one was around. I looked into a couple of empty offices but didn't see any directories. As I was peering around, a woman in a blue suit came up to us.

"Can I help you?" she asked suspiciously.

"No thank you," I answered as Rose pressed the elevator call button.

"Who are you looking for?" she demanded, her voice rising. "And who are you people?"

"We have an appointment with Kathy," Rose said unfazed. My heart was leaping to my throat and I was already sweating.

"I'm Kathy Simpson," she answered, "and I'm not expecting anyone."

Rose tugged me into the crowd in the elevator that just opened behind us.

"We're sorry," she called to the woman. "We were looking for Kathy Karos."

But the woman was suspicious. She came towards the elevator saying, "Stop," but the door closed and we stood uncomfortably in the group staring at us.

"She's so difficult," said Rose, fuming as if the two of them had an ongoing feud. A woman standing behind us said, "I'm not going to miss that pill."

Rose pressed six and when the door open there was a crowd so she pressed five saying, "Oops, my mind isn't what it used to be."

"I'm that way lately," I said as if sympathizing. I couldn't believe her sangfroid.

When the door opened on five it looked empty so we got off and I breathed a sigh. We were not completely alone however. Others were still leaving. I casually bought a coke from the machine by the elevator bank.

"Oh good," said Rose loudly, "at least the one on this floor is working. Get me a Pepsi."

When the coast was clear we walked toward the dark end of the floor of five-foot high cubicles.

"Get down," Rose told me, and we crawled down an aisle on our knees. I saw a book on the desk of the first partition and grabbed it, but it was someone's datebook so I put it on the floor. Rose pointed down the hall at the farthest desk, which was larger than the others. I crawled over to it. There were a couple of people talking around the corner as I leaned into the partition and carefully opened the left hand drawer of the desk.

Sure enough, the book I grabbed was the Internal Directory. I held it to my chest and edged backwards to Rose and we were on our feet just in time for the couple of employees who were talking to come around the corner.

"She went for the idea," I improvised, as if discussing old business. "We'll have it ready by Tuesday."

Hermes the Spy was with us both now. The two people held the elevator door as Rose and I continued a bogus conversation for a moment, then stopped to appear polite in an elevator.

When we got to the lobby the tall security officer was talking to Kathy Simpson but luckily they had their backs to us so we walked through the turnstile behind the departing employees looking as nonchalant as possible.

"If you look at him he'll feel our glance," Rose whispered as we walked to the street.

"You're terrifying," I said in the plaza, my heart still racing. Rose burst out in a joyful little scream.

"Just give me M to Z like we agreed," she said when she caught her breath.

"You're remarkable."

"You have to make your own good luck," she scoffed.

I opened up twenty accounts from that list and Rose opened thirty.

"You think that list is something," said Big Nose. "Wolf told me he went out during a ticker tape parade and collected client statements right off the sidewalk."

"Still," he added, "you shouldn't be hanging out with that broad."

"Gluck said to follow the producers."

"Yeah, right into jail," he said, shaking his head. "I know how to handle women. You have to keep them guessing. I got this broad in Jersey City who cuts my hair and does my laundry and while that's running she gives me a blowjob."

"A full service station."

"I told her I was married so she wouldn't get any ideas."

"How romantic."

"Women aren't romantic," he began, waxing into his version of philosophical Apollo. "Men are romantic. Women are realists. They just want you to think the opposite because they live in their feelings, but that's not romantic. Romantic means wanting to conquer mountains, take on risks, come work on Wall Street. Men like dreaming, roaming, and daring the uncertainties of life. You know what women want? They want tomorrow."

"What do you mean?"

"They want guarantees. They'll marry a so-so looking guy if he can provide for them and call it love because he isn't hot. They don't care about writing poetry like you do—"

"There are plenty of women poets," I protested, "starting with Sappho."

"Rose is the most romantic woman I've ever met," he said abruptly.

I hadn't considered this but she was a dreamer and a risk-taker even if she was crude.

"She's the next step in evolution," he continued, "the one who's going to eat mankind."

By his logic I was a romantic because I kept pursuing sexual adventures at the booth store, which was all I had time for. I got careless one night and burned my nostrils with poppers.

Rose took one look and laughed. At the end of the day she gave me some pointers.

"You have to hold them away from your nose, silly faggot," she said warmly. "Or at least put Vaseline on your nose first."

I froze.

"You think you're fooling me?" she asked incredulously. Then she smiled winningly. "Nothing can shock me. Men are pigs. We're all pigs."

I went into the mailroom, reached into my pants, and pulled off the metal cock ring I was wearing that day in honor of Hermes and handed it to Rose.

"What is this?" she asked, turning it over in her hands. "It's warm, why is it warm?"

I laughed. She dropped it on the floor with a little scream.

"I thought nothing could shock you!"

"We're all pigs," she said, giving a belly laugh.

"It takes a pig to satisfy a pig," said Big Nose, staring at her.

"This job makes me so horny," said Rose, staring back at him and pulling her skirt down to cover her legs.

"Want me to call my girlfriend and get her to talk dirty?" he asked.

"The 'real estate brawd' as you call her in that low class accent of yours?"

"None of his girlfriends have names," I informed her.

"I got this one tamed," he began. "She picked me up at the airport when I flew back from Florida with a bottle of champagne. Then she's sucking my dick while I'm driving the car right through the tollbooth and swigging out of the bottle. I got this broad's head in my lap bobbing up and down while I hand the guy the three bucks."

"Did he say anything?"

"What the fuck does he care? Maybe his job is so dull he doesn't see anything. Now don't talk," he said dialing. He told his girlfriend that he was alone at the office and then put her on speakerphone whenever she spoke.

"Play with yourself," he told her. "Pretend I'm down there doing you under the desk."

I blushed and Rose rolled her eyes.

"I'm all wet," she said over the speaker.

Wolf came over and quickly grasped the situation.

"Fucking perverts," he said. Big Nose held his finger to his lips to shush him but it was too late.

"Am I on speaker phone?" the voice demanded and then she heard us guffaw.

"I'm really on speaker phone," she shouted, "you put me on the speaker."

Big Nose picked up the phone and began apologizing and then he laughed.

"She says it was hot and I should come by tonight," he said, basking in our admiration. "See, I know the fine art of living."

"Takes money," said Wolf.

"Takes time more than money," said Big Nose. "You have to make time for the essentials of life like the gym and blowjobs. You can't spend all your time chasing money. Don't you hear that word 'spend'? You only got so much time to spend in one life and sex should be one of your major purchases."

"Oh yeah?" said Wolf. "Is that your version of taking time to smell the roses?"

Big Nose looked at Rose and said, "Sure I smell her, don't you?"

Rose hit him over the head affectionately with the research brochure in her hands.

"Money is the great amplifier," continued Big Nose, his voice back in philosophical Apollo. "Whatever your character, it's more so with money. Money shows you how people would live if they were free."

"So if you had a fatter wallet you'd be seducing younger women?" asked Rose.

"I heard that bitch," came the Real Estate Brawd's voice over the speakerphone, but she didn't really sound offended.

"They wouldn't just be after me for my tall, dark body and huge dick," he answered.

"Yeah baby," said the voice over the speaker. "He's fucking huge you guys."

"I don't want to hear about it," said Wolf with disgust.

"Thanks, Hon," said Big Nose, delighted to scandal us. "Tell them about how you came in one Saturday when no one was here and I banged you in the bathroom while you signed the margin agreement."

"That was so hot baby."

"I just leaned her against the sink and fucked her while she signed on the dotted line."

"Oh yeah," came the voice over the speaker, "that's what they call sealing the deal."

"I'll see you tonight late and you can have all you want," he told her, and hung up when she agreed.

"I agree that you're tall and dark," said Rose, "I have yet to see proof of the rest."

"I'll show you mine if you show me yours and we'll see who's bigger, Rose," he offered, reaching for his zipper.

"Please don't," Wolf said abruptly. Then he brightened up.

"Why don't we go have some brews at the Athletic Club tonight over billiards? I've got cigars."

"Boys night out?" said Rose. "That's an all-male gym."

"I can sneak you in," he said. "You can wear my trench coat and hat. Anyway they know me there and I've smuggled girls in before. Just don't make a fuss please."

"I'm a woman not a girl," said Rose, sticking her chest out as I watched Big Nose's eyes widen.

"I say you're Warrior Aphrodite," I said.

"I'm hot," she admitted, "if that's what you mean."

The club looked more like a palace than a gym. I could smell the pool in the foyer, which was richly decorated with carpets and tooled green leather walls.

The billiards room was a jewel box encrusted with Victorian décor under vaulting and heavy beams. I looked at the billiard table and felt sheepish, for I had never played. I tried to beg off and fancied myself smoking a cigar and watching thoughtfully like some wise uncle on one of the quilted green leather chairs along the side but the others weren't going to have it.

"So you'll suck at it. Who's surprised?" asked Wolf, aiming a cue expertly over his rolled up sleeves and holding an unlit cigar in his teeth. "It doesn't say anything about you as a person or prove that you're a homo," he added, as he continued to hit every shot and moved around the table like a predator.

After a few rounds of beer and much peering over the low lighting of the billiard table, Wolf put his arm over my shoulder. I cringed.

"Hey, Michael," he said to me, already drunk, "are you male bonding tonight? Is this a meaningful breakthrough for you? Are you going to bang on your drum tonight or bang on whatever? Or are you the one who gets banged?"

He was so handsome in a perfect, Apollo way that it made his viciousness all the more biting. I tried to remember that he was drunk and that Dionysus was doing the talking, but I knew that *wine gives a look-see into a man,* as the Greeks said.

"I've known butcher guys than you," I answered.

"I bet you have," he said. "You know, we'd all respect you more if you'd just admit you're gay and stop pretending, because there's nothing worse than a phony."

Big Nose and Rose looked at me.

"Are you asking me out?"

"Michael," he asked defiantly, "Have you ever put a gerbil up your ass?"

The waiter came by during this question but registered nothing.

"That's not gay and you're not funny."

"Sir," he told the man standing waiting for orders, "Bring this young gerbil killer another beer. I'll take a Tom Collins." He seemed accustomed to being served.

"Did I ever tell you about the anonymous shitter?" he asked as he gulped his fifth cocktail. He was getting pretty drunk. "There was this guy in college, someone on the swim team, who used to take a dump on the end of the diving board at night. We'd open up the pool for the morning swim and there'd be this big lump of shit at the end of the diving board."

"Fess up, Wolf," said Rose, "You did it."

"We never figured out who it was. But can you imagine what's going on in someone's mind while he's taking a dump squatting on the end of the diving board?" he laughed. "Imagine him grinning like some dog, squatting and shitting naked on the wobbly board? And then of course you have to tiptoe backwards so you don't spring it off the board."

"You must have pretty good balance," said Rose.

The waiter came back with his cocktail. Wolf drank half of it while the man stood there.

"One more," he said, "And put everything on my tab."

We thanked him for the treat.

"You have to be invited to join this club by two different members," observed Big Nose, "Any blacks here yet besides as staff?"

"It does seem pretty white around here," said Rose, admiring the room.

"The men swim naked here," I said. "I've heard about it."

"Of course you have," said Wolf, putting his arm over my shoulder once more and giving me a strange smile. I cringed. He was leaning heavily on me.

When our glasses were empty, we headed outside, the looming darkness of Central Park confronting us like a living presence.

"Let's go for a walk in the Park," said Wolf, stumbling and leaning now against Big Nose.

"Naw, I'm gonna get you into this cab," he said, opening the door of the taxi waiting outside the club and helping Wolf inside.

"I'm going to take the train," I said, knowing that no one else was heading downtown.

"You've had a few, too, Mike," said Big Nose.

"Not as many as our buddy," I answered and waved him off.

I left Rose and Big Nose on the sidewalk and headed towards Eighth Avenue, but instead of going into the subway, I crossed over the Central Park West and walked uptown alongside the Park. At 72nd Street I turned into the Park, following a trail that led up towards the Rambles, the notorious gay cruising area. As I left the Avenue behind me, the city hovered dreamlike above the treetops, the buildings bathed in light beyond the local darkness and receding into the distance like my sober self. I trudged across a small clearing in the ambiguous light and then turned down a path that plunged into thick woods. I kept thinking I saw movement in the trees but it was the shadows of trunks moving in relation to my own movement. Benches cropped up in the moonlight and then I came upon a statue of a runner, posed like Hermes in a full pace.

With too many drinks in me, Dionysus filled me with imaginary fears. At any moment, a mugger might show himself from behind the bushes or I might stumble across a dead body, but I had enough Athena left in me at the time to know I was intoxicated and to keep the god at bay. Besides, I knew that the fog hid me from danger as much as it hid danger from me.

The light mist became a heavy fog as I walked steadily downhill through the complex winding paths. The dull roar of traffic sounded like the distant ocean. The darkness was thick and yet I knew I was not alone. The Park is never really empty.

The incoming fog quickly blotted out the sky, making everything seem near as I heard a strange noise in the branches ahead of me, a dull hum.

It was a homeless man snoring on a park bench. A plastic bottle of Vodka lay on the ground beside him. I continued along the path into the Rambles.

Human forms appeared on either side of me, lurching towards and then away from me along the path in the fog. I slowed down, fascinated and intrigued by this crossroads of

Hermes like the ancient meeting places. I passed a few individuals fairly close by but the thick darkness concealed their faces. It was like walking among the dead.

There were muffled sounds of speech but none of it was intelligible. I stepped off the main path and wandered into the small overgrown woods. Men were standing everywhere looming towards each other. One man pulled mechanically at his crotch as he stood on the path under the streetlight which was a dull glare floating over the fog.

I saw an athletic looking young man in a hoodie standing by the side of the path and I veered towards him, but when I got close instead of Eros peeking out of his hood, I saw a look of pleading and hunger. Eros' children are Want and Need, but this was no place to satisfy either of them. I felt chilled when he touched my shoulder and pushed him away, walking out of that Underworld until I came to an empty clearing.

There was a dark figure standing in front of me by some bushes. He raised his hand and said, "Excuse me sir, do you know what time it is?"

Athena's armor instantly went up. I knew this wasn't right. Why would someone in this situation ask me the time of day? Immediately two other men appeared from behind the bushes and I started to run. My heart was in my throat as I ran like prey towards the Avenue with the three of them on my heels and gaining. Just in time I came out on Central Park West and ran out into the street in front of a cab, holding my arms out in emergency fashion.

I jumped into the cab. My pursuers stood on the sidewalk and watched us pull away. One of them lit a cigarette.

Wolf sulked the next day with a hangover. He wore his sunglasses at his desk and kept quiet all day. His face radiated the same white innocence as ever. No one said a word about the night before.

Gorgons

A rising tide lifts all boats.

We were constantly bailed out of the most hopeless situations by the raging bull market. The animal spirits of Poseidon, the Bull God, drove the public into stocks in herds.

You could pick almost any stock and it would eventually go up. Fortune had us riding high on her wheel.

"The business of America is business" was the collective mantra. The statue of Liberty in the harbor holding aloft her torch proclaimed the will and power of the Almighty Dollar like Athena proclaiming the ascendancy of her city-state. America's complexity and depth manifested in the Market, an enchanting and unpredictable goddess whose moods were divined by her many priests and oracles of stock analysis and economics, but she remained an unfathomable goddess, perverse in her constant reversals and prone like the Underworld gods to bring about what is most dreaded or least expected in her rebellion against predictability.

She was an Earth Mother in her abundance and subject to the seasons. The January Effect brings a new start in small caps, as the New Year brings in fresh 401K contributions and the cash flows in through spring like melting snow. April brings stormy weather as the new heights and hopes consolidate or rotate to other sectors, spreading the fertile mud. Green growth is pruned at tax season but this only makes room for fresh monies and later blooms.

"Sell in May then go away." The end of the spring rain prepares the sacrifices of the June solstice that sets up the inevitable summer rally.

Fall starts in mid-August with the first chill of the winter sell-off. Downdrafts blow investors between the greed of un-reaped gains and the school day return of Zeus' harsh reality. Stocks fall with the leaves into Demeter's harvest festival of Thanksgiving, sacred to the Family Self, which counts down the days till the return of the Wise King Chronos, God of the Golden Days and spending sprees, whose American double is Santa Claus. The strange days between Christmas and New Year's mark a time out of time with light volume levitating stocks that will be pounded down again in early January only to start the cycle once more.

The summer of '87 had a heady run. If you didn't invest now you would miss your last chance. Prophets spoke of 'unbundling' equities to expose their hidden values in assets and earnings power in a new paradigm that changed everything. This was a mythic period of wealth creation to be rued in old age by those who didn't act before it was too late.

"Things have changed' was proclaimed high and low on the Street as the gods drove on the collective hubris to its impious head. Ayn Rand's Olympians had triumphed over the dark forces of cyclical downturns and bear markets. Only fools who wanted to waste their lives waiting for bargains were out of the market. We were entering uncharted waters, a new era of shared prosperity, an unclaimed virgin land to the west where the riches and ripe fruit of Elysium beckoned by the setting sun.

During the summer of '87, Carnival Cruise Line had its Initial Public Offering and for once there was a hot IPO with plenty of shares to go around. I got the whole office singing the Carnival Cruise song: "In the morning, in the evening, Carnival's got the fun" in my best Kathy Lee imitation. We were all on a high because it was so easy to open accounts on the stock. All you had to do was call a travel agent and say, "Your ship has come in."

But the gods were watching angrily.

The first gusts of cool air in September brought in an unusual spirit of doubt and reflection. Athena's judgment was starting to turn against stocks. Earnings had peaked, rates were rising, and it looked like the best was behind us. Hurricane season brought an ominous tone as the trade deficit, bloated by the strong dollar and years of consumer spending on imports, menaced an ocean of red ink. Bond yields, stretched by rampant government spending, broached ten percent, a very appealing alternative to the risks of equities.

People acted strangely to the new level of stress. The older brokers were whispering to each other. Phil Way, the cold-calling shark from Lehman, started standing in his office while he dialed with an endless coffee in his hand. He seemed strangely animated.

"Do you think it's coke?" I asked Big Nose after I saw him gesticulating wildly in his room.

A few days later, Gluck called an impromptu meeting for Phil to present an options strategy for this turbulent market.

"Two out of three options expire worthless," Wolf announced as we crowded around the conference desk waiting for Phil. "So the best strategy is to sell covered calls, which is safe enough even for LOL's. The rest is a waste of time and too risky," he muttered.

"Sorry I'm late," said Way as he rushed into the room with his hair disheveled.

"Markets like these are good for spreads," he began. Then he described a series of options strategies but in such a manic way that patronizing smiles started forming and when I caught Big Nose's eye he winked. Phil's hands were shaking, he was sniffing, and his jaw kept opening and closing compulsively like a shark. After a few minutes of his wandering speech Gluck interrupted him and thanked him and told us to get back to work.

"Phil, would you come by my office?" he said, looking pained as we filed out of the conference room.

He stood before the boss' desk wiping his brow. When he emerged, Gluck told him to "go home for the day and come back fresh tomorrow". He wasn't going to let his pet shark go easily.

Older brokers were fearful about the Market. 'Don't fight the Fed', 'Don't fight the Tape', and 'Don't catch a falling knife'--they repeated the ancient curses to us young upstarts who had never seen a bear market before. October began with choppiness and unheard of daily swings of volatility.

"This is a healthy and long overdue correction," I assured my clients, "and we should take advantage of these bargain prices."

That worked for a trade or two but when those trades also went south the money dried up because *averaging down is like re-arranging deck chairs on the Titanic.* Days of one hundred point drops became more frequent as terrified Icarus realized his wings were melting. Pools of capital fled to cash when even the safety of money markets was called into question. The Furies prepared to mete out their implacable judgment as we saw beloved stocks at prices as shocking as naked pictures of family members. Technicians spoke ominously about three black crows as we closed three days in a row at lower lows on increasingly heavy volume.

The last market day before the Crash was a Friday. I opened a new account on a hundred shares of Toys R Us. Gluck paused in front of my glass partition to listen in as I took down the account information.

"That was a good pitch, " he said, "But how much more difficult is it to say 'a thousand shares' than 'a hundred shares'?"

"Are you going to cover me if she doesn't pay?"

He cracked a mischievous smile and walked off.

After market Big Nose, Rose, and I went for drinks at the Riviera Café in the Village to watch passersby. There were the usual tourists and gay men cruising but even on that beautiful afternoon in the setting sun, a pall hung over the crowd. The good times had lasted too long.

Over the weekend I picked up a copy of the financial classic, "Reminiscences of a Stock Operator", a retelling of the Crash of '29, and pictured myself driving a cab to save my job on Wall Street and telling the young folk how lucky they were to have missed that accursed era.

Meanwhile the media feasted on the prospect of global ruin. By Monday morning the bottom fell out of Hong Kong, Tokyo, and London.

"Do not take lunch," Gluck proclaimed at an emergency meeting before the bell. "Do not bottom fish. Do not try to outsmart the Market. I don't want any checks for new accounts unless they're certified because there's going to be a feeding frenzy of renegs."

I bit my nails as the ticker spelled out our fate like a terrible diagnosis. Nemesis was having her day as we went down sharply in the morning and then stabilized over lunch through the bulls' last stand, but the outflow was not to be stanched. My face was gleaming with sweat. Once traders start drawing lines in the sand and saying that a certain level must hold it's already too late, because Fear has replaced Greed as Fortune's Wheel turns round.

The bears were back at two with a Rebel yell as one century-mark after another toppled into a whirlpool of selling like waves wiping out a sand castle. Everyone was calling his broker and getting out at any price. Customers calling for reassurance could only sit out the storm or take untenable losses. "It's over," I said to the screen, shaking my head as the panic destroyed our financial crops like a swarm of locusts. All the profits were gone and everything was a loss.

At four o'clock we went to Harry's. The sidewalk reeled with young men in suits holding plastic cups of beer. An old broker who looked like Uncle Sam in a pinstripe suit pointed an angry finger at us as he leaned on his carved wooden cane.

"You Yuppies did this to us!" he rasped. "Now you've brought down the whole house around you. Your optimism was arrogance."

He was a comic little figure like a puppet in his blue pin.

"I didn't know Death had a day job," said Big Nose.

The old guy bought us drinks.

"C'mon boys," he croaked cheerfully, "May as well drink up. You're going to need it. Welcome to the world of us mortals."

Uncle Sam treated us to a number of rounds so we got drunk pretty fast on our empty stomachs. Big Nose was leaning heavily on my shoulder.

"Why don't you give the old guy a hug?" I told him.

"You want me to kiss him, too?" he said, going over to the guy and giving him a loud kiss on the cheek. The two of them were laughing and chatting like old friends.

"Hey this Uncle Sam is all right," said Big Nose, smiling with his arm over the old guy's shoulder. "C'mon, Injun Rose, give the old guy a peck on the cheek," and she surprised all of us—including the old guy--by giving him a real kiss on the mouth.

The Crash only lasted a day but it ambushed our future like the War God slaying the troops as they sleep. Where once there was complacency and planning, Hekate, the witch of Hades, emerged as the eerie unreality of the days that followed. The world was turned upside down and things could quickly get worse. Soothsayers and crackpots predicting further Apocalypse popped up on the media claiming to have *told you so* all along. The commissions ran up briefly with liquidations but it was blood money as people got out of the market at any price.

"You make money whether I buy or sell," said Mr. Jones. "What do you care?"

"Are you going to buy anything else from me again?"

The new account that bought Toys R Us called me anxious to know whether or not I had received her check.

"Yes."

"Damn it," she said. "It's cashed already."

"Were you going to stick me with the trade?"

"You folks have deep pockets," said the sweet elderly lady with the bed-and-breakfast in Vermont, sounding offended.

Soon the joke went around the office that "DUIT blew it". It was gallows humor, like Hermes joking as he leads the dead down to eternal rest. The buying panic quickly dried up into a terrible silence, the kind that follows disaster. The telephones were quiet and people whispered as though the office was a museum--everyone except Big Nose, who seemed energized by the destruction around him like Persephone, the Underworld Goddess, clearing the air.

"The credit card economy is over," he said with strange satisfaction. "No more twenty-five year olds driving Jags and sniffing coke in the men's room. All the Lehman sharks are going down the toilet. I can breathe again."

Phil Way lost the firm a fortune in uncovered options and margin calls and didn't show up again.

"The cold caller's gone cold."

"What are you, a Socialist?" asked Rose.

"Someone has to give a shit, Rose," he said, "Or don't you want your relatives to have a place to immigrate to?"

"And how are we going to survive?"

"There's life insurance and disability," he answered. "It's not as sexy as stocks but the premiums are great. A ten thousand dollar investment puts four in your pocket and the customer never even feels it. Call the men with families. Worry sells. 'Mr. Jones, what will you do, what will you do?'" he said in a scary Halloween voice.

"How much does the Bogey Man make?"

"I'd rather die than sell insurance," I said.

"Dying's cheap," he answered. "Being unable to work is expensive. You should call all your artist types with a disability policy before they can't buy it at all, if you catch my drift."

I pretended not to know what he was talking about but I took out the maximum coverage when the firm offered upgrades, which they did every time they changed the name on the door. I worked for EF Hutton, Shearson Lehman,

American Express, Citibank, and Morgan Stanley—all without changing desks.

At the sales meeting, Gluck gestured frenetically.

"In markets like these you have keep your nose clean," he warned us. "Nothing shady, nothing not fully on the up-and-up. Get all the legal documents in and get real signatures, no more signing client agreements for each other because that is coming back to bite us in the butt."

"You can't stick your head in the sand because while you're craning your neck down there you're going to see six attorneys looking back up at you from Hell where they all come from. The Fed's dying to give the public satisfaction. Everyone wants blood."

"Look," he said consolingly, "you can hurt the little guy, the schmoe with only ten or twenty thousand, but you can't hurt the big guy. In markets like these you'll lose the little guy anyway. But the business-owner, the surgeon, the ones with the cash flowing in—they are your future, so watch out for them and set your priorities. If you can keep one guy worth ten Carnival Cruise accounts then you'll have a lot less work."

I had expected the usual berating sales talk given how bad business was. I soon learned the reason for this unusual benignity.

Everyone was leaving the firm. Headhunters were scooping up brokers with bonuses based on last year's production because they wanted the assets in house. Everyone burned his book but there was still equity in a list because some of those people will come back and a stock crash primes them to start from scratch with someone else.

Within two months we went from sixty brokers to twenty-two. Most went to other firms but others left the business entirely, burnt out and ready for something else.

"It's Christmas time all over the Earth," sang Wolf as he and Gluck distributed accounts. There were more than anyone could handle. They didn't even have time to pick them over properly.

"Now I don't want you saying anything negative about anyone who left," Gluck instructed us, "like 'He was a great guy; it's tragic how drugs took over his life' or, 'I didn't like his girlfriends or his boyfriends', because a lot of these guys are friends with their accounts and you'll only disparage the firm. Talk to them about their relationship with the firm and don't even mention the broker. He never existed, okay?"

The Crash was actually good for us younger brokers because of this new account bonanza. Persephone's destructive vengeance left opportunity in its wake and I inherited hundreds of accounts with ten million in assets, bringing my asset base to over twenty million. Rose and Big Nose fared equally well. It was a holy feast in the office for us.

"You guys are so lucky," said Jill, emerging from her leafy office. "You're just starting out. You haven't burnt your books. Your clients don't hate you." She leaned against my desk looking pained.

"Just four months ago, I was making over two hundred thousand dollars a year and now I'll be lucky to make half that. I took the money for granted and now it's just stopped coming in. Of course, I was an idiot and didn't save a penny. I had to shop like a crazy woman," she said, rolling her eyes and adding comically, "Because I'm worth it!"

"Yes, Hera darling," I said, "you are the queen."

The downswing of Fortunes' wheel left the older brokers walking around like zombies, shaking their heads and whispering to each other.

The week before Christmas, I was walking to the bathroom when I noticed Coffin hunched over his desk, his head resting on his hands. I'd never seen him taking a nap before so when I saw him still hunched over on my way back, I approached his glass partition and tapped.

No answer. I went in and shook his shoulder, and his head fell off his elbows onto the desk with a thud. His eyes were open and blank as puddles. I ran into Gluck's office.

"Ok," he said with remarkable coolness. "Turn the light off in that office and go back to your desk. I'll handle the rest."

A stretcher quietly took him out of the office while people gathered around sniffing into tissues.

"I can't believe it," said Big Nose. "He was looking great ever since he stopped managing the office. He had gone back to playing tennis. He never smoked. I don't get it."

"There's no preparing for death," said Rose, looking off in the distance, "It's always a surprise no matter how old you are or how much you think about it."

By noon, you wouldn't know that Coffin ever worked there. The posters were down and the photos and desk knickknacks were collected and put into a box for his family.

I felt so empty looking at the room stripped of its humanity that I fetched a couple dozen white tulips from the florist down the street and strewed them around the room--on the desk, the floor, the chair--as a ritual gesture.

"That is so touching," Jill sobbed. "White tulips, where did you learn that?"

The next morning, we piled into the black cars headed for the noon service in Brooklyn. I sat up front in the cab with Gluck, Wolf and Big Nose in the back. At first we kept a respectful silence, burning with the sting of mortality. It was stifling so I opened the window a crack.

The thin breeze smelled vaguely of the ocean. Gluck spoke first.

"I know you were counting on getting his accounts but we have to distribute most of them or there'll be squawking. When we get back, go through them and separate the top twenty and the next fifty. You can split the second group with Jill."

They shared a knowing smile.

"What about Fester?" said Wolf. "She's his daughter-in-law and might have fantasies about coming back."

"Fester isn't coming back," said Gluck firmly. "Don't worry about her. She can twirl her nipples all she wants but it's going to remain a fantasy."

They guffawed at the image and Big Nose and I felt obliged to laugh with them.

This reminded the boss that we were in the car with them.

"And throw them a couple of bones," he added, looking us over thoughtfully.

"They took my Ben away!" screamed his old widow at the wake, weeping hysterically and looking around like a terrified animal seeking refuge. The other mourners watched, respectful and horrified into silence.

"They took him away from me, Wolf," she said, rushing over to hug him. She reeked of alcohol. "They took his dead body, just like that, my Ben's body after fifty-five years together. He went to work and they took his body and put him in a box and now they're burying him in the dirt. Just like that. He was with me last night, Wolf. We made love together like we did every Sunday night since always. I called him at the office yesterday to ask him what he wanted for dinner and they put you on the phone, Wolf. He was old but he was still fit and healthy and he didn't have that office to worry about anymore. Now they took him away in a box forever. And I wasn't there to say goodbye. Where was God in all this? Where the hell was God, Wolf?"

He held her and tears welled in his eyes.

"Where the fuck was God?" she shouted, looking wildly around the room.

"Pretty bleak," I whispered to Big Nose and Rose while Fester and some other women hovered around the widow weeping and consoling.

"No one knows what happens when you die," said Rose, "But I suspect that white light they talk about is just the last brain cell signing off like when you win at solitaire and get all the fancy graphics. Otherwise the whole human race would have committed suicide a long time ago."

"Heaven isn't worth the wait," said Big Nose simply.

Back at the office, Gluck held another meeting.

"You're not going to hear this from me very often, but it's important for you to take care of yourselves. Take a vacation every now and then. Reward yourself when you're doing well. Get a massage. Take up a sport. If work is going well and your customers are happy, take a week off and let your partner cover your accounts. You owe it to yourself to spend some money because what's the point otherwise? Now don't ever expect to hear this from me again."

A grim chuckle traversed the room.

That afternoon, I received my bone for witnessing the sordid discussion about Coffin's accounts. Alex Andropocitch was in his eighties and owned a deli on the Lower East Side. He had saved over a million dollars worth of stocks.

"I started investing in America before I met Ben," he told me in a strong Yiddish accent. "I told him 'Ben, you're not going to make a fortune off me because I'm going to buy and hold forever. So pick good blue chips and call me every six months with more and I'll keep on adding. Andereweise, I can go to the races if I feel like losing money."

"Verstanden," I said, risking my German, which he might find offensive.

"Unglaublich," he said with delight. "I've got a Yiddish speaking broker. But you have an Irish name. You have to come in sometime and meet my granddaughter. You got a shiksa?"

"Sorta," I stumbled. I wasn't about to correct his taking me for Irish, since there was no knowing how he'd like my Syrian background and I was already in like Flynn.

"No trouble," he said. "But I like you already and wouldn't mind an Irish for a son-in-law. Come in have a

sandwich sometime. We got the greatest liverwurst in town"—
which he pronounced 'liverwoist'. "And a bottomless pickle
barrel."

"How's your pastrami?"

"Only hands down the best in town," he recited what
must have been an advertising slogan. "We have the awards
to prove it, too."

As winter deepened, the market volume dried up like
an ancient sea turning to desert. We were stuck in the horse
latitudes, a tight trading range that made it impossible to make
a living.

I had few expenses so I lived low and maintained a
vigil, waiting for more favorable markets to return like the gods
of spring.

Big Nose saw my scrapes in the locker room when I
was changing.

"What the fuck are you doing to yourself?" he asked,
pointing at the scabs. Then he pointed to a purple mark on
the back of my calf that I hadn't noticed.

"Looks like you missed one," he said. "You really ought to go to the doctor and get that checked. It's not normal."

I pretended to ignore him because I didn't want to talk about it. The only drug out was AZT and that had mixed reviews at best so I just didn't want to know. Hades and his illness and death would have to wait.

Our workouts took on a new passion, fueled by Ares' fight and determination. I got up to 195 pounds of solid muscle with a thirty-inch waist and a forty-four chest. Big Nose was beaming, "Look at my creation."

I got in an hour before him to do my abs routine and sprints. Looking at myself in the mirror as I swooped up and down in the Roman chair with my t-shirt pulled up to see the fettuccini obliques, I looked too good to be sick. Things were going too well in my life for me to be sick. Most of all, I didn't have time to be sick. Ate's Blindness possessed me like a cloud of fog sitting around my shoulders.

When the office started Casual Fridays, I was bursting out of my Polo.

"Look at those guns!" said Big Nose, pointing at my arms. "Sorry to bust bawls around here but most of you guys look like suburban sprawl."

"You gym homos look great," sneered Wolf, whose belly had grown noticeably since he got married.

During the next couple of months, the purple spots moved up from my calves to my thighs, then onto my waist and stomach. A few showed up on my arms. I changed into my gym sweats in the bathroom stall at the office and showered at home to hide them from Big Nose, and I turned the dimmer down low in the shower and pulled off my jeans under the covers to hide them from myself. I was far beyond the intervention of the butter knife.

Business got so slow that Gluck called an urgent meeting.

"You people are shit," he ranted like an angry Zeus. "You aren't salesmen. You do lousy when the market does lousy. You have to be better than the market."

As he went on with his tirade, my heart began to break and I wiped my face against my sleeve. When I looked up my watery eyes met Jill's and her eyes got wet, too. When the meeting ended she grabbed my arm and pulled me into the elevator.

"Let's get some air," she said gently as the doors closed. As we descended I remembered how I used to dream about falling. Sometimes this dream happened as a daydream and the whole world became strange and seemed to slide off at a strange angle and become uncanny for a moment as if I didn't know who or what I was. I called these moments my *visits to Hades*.

She led me to one of the black marble benches lining the low black pool in our lobby with the phallic pillars on balls around the perimeter. I wept openly, choking softly in rhythm on Jill's shoulder.

"He's such a beast," she said. "He shouldn't try to motivate people by yelling at them," and then, looking into my face, "You are so sensitive, Michael. I've never known a man who was so free with his emotions."

"I'm a big baby."

"At least you've got feelings, which is more than I can say about most of these lugs."

She sat with me quietly while I calmed down.

"Michael," she said, her voice becoming solemn. "There's something I want to discuss with you. I've been thinking about leaving the business and I'd like you to take over my accounts."

I sat still as a frightened deer, not believing my ears.

"I know that if someone said that to me when I was in your position, I would have died of joy," she said, reprimanding my silence. "I want to go work with my father and help him with his money management accounts. My sister has been working there for five years and his health is failing, I'm sorry to say. I don't see why she should get all the business if something happens to him, so I've got to get in there and get to know the clients."

"I am very grateful and honored," I said, light years away from the person who was sobbing a moment before. That was Psyche in despair; now Hermes the Opportunist was sitting on my bench.

She put her hand on my knee in earnest.

"I'm not sure how it will work out, so what I'd like to do is make you my partner first. If I just left cold there'd be no coming back. Once the partnership is set up it can't be revoked so this is a big step for me. You will share my clients but you can keep your own business. I'll take fifty percent of the commissions that you generate with my accounts and when it works out with my dad I'll leave you the whole thing."

I was reeling and trying not to let her know it.

"It's a good arrangement for me and an incredible opportunity for you. I worked too hard to just hand these accounts over to the office and let those monsters swallow them up in two minutes. I think you're the kind of sensitive soul my accounts deserve."

"I am honest," I offered, convincing because it was true.

"Once you know the customers," she said, "they're virtually yours, because you'll be working with them daily. I'll look over the commission run of course to confirm that you are trading in our joint number. I want you to know that I chose you for my partner, Michael, because there are so few people here I can trust."

I thought of the incident with the old lady and Becker when Jill said I had to give him back the account and shrugged.

"I have to tell you," she said, "that I chose you against Gluck's recommendation."

"Who did he want?"

"Rose."

"She's a cannibal."

"Michael, one more thing. I'd like to get something on the table. Are you gay?"

I hesitated. There was no point in denying it since she seemed to see right through me and I seemed to unconsciously announce it to the world.

"Yes."

"I thought so. If I were ten years younger, I would probably have been a lesbian. Your generation did the gay thing while mine did drugs. I was a dancer after college and met a lot of gay men so it's cool with me--it's great with me-- but I wouldn't broadcast it to the office if I were you. People who are cool to that sort of thing will know anyway, but I'm not sure what Gluck would think."

"Gluck doesn't like gays?"

"I don't know," she said with a look of concern, "but I know Wolf doesn't and he's his right hand man."

"There is a gay ordinance in the city that protects me."

"Try to prove that when he fires you," she retorted. "In this business, the manager can do whatever he wants. Don't forget that. It's important for you to remember that."

She peered at me as she said this.

I stared at the fountain. The water dribbled slowly over the low, black granite edges into the little gully.

"You wouldn't want to lose your credibility with the accounts, would you?" she asked me. "I know you're honest but please promise to act in their best interest and not just squeeze commissions out of them."

"That I can promise."

"I've been buying them limited partnerships because I can't deal with price fluctuations but now since the Crash those are all worthless and I'm screwed. At least they show up on the statement at the original investment price, but that won't last forever."

She was referring to oil and gas partnerships like America First and real estate partnerships like the ones Jim used to put together. They all had conservative sounding names to reassure the old folks and drape their shady deals in the flag.

"We'll split roles," she said. "I don't have the stomach to sell stocks so that will be your side of the business. I'll be the bond lady and come in on Fridays just to do bonds and keep an eye on things."

"Agreed," I said, "and thank you, Jill. Thank you from the bottom of my heart."

I meant it. When I moved to shake her hand, she grabbed my shoulders and kissed me French style on both cheeks, smiling.

"Are you coming back upstairs?" she asked, walking towards the elevators.

"I'm going to take a walk in the park now and absorb this," I told her. "It's a lot."

Jill was granting me the favor of a lifetime but she also had something on me, something Gluck wouldn't like.

It was a beautiful day in April. The Battery was thronged with tourists waiting for the ferry to the Statue of Liberty. I passed them in my blue suit playing the jaded New Yorker. The harbor was busy with boats plying the fine weather.

Now I would have a real income in this fabulous city. I could live a normal, suburban life of comfort right in the thick of things.

I bought a bag of peanuts from the umbrella stand and entered the massive fortress of Castle Clinton. Inside, the birds flitted among their roosts in the eaves, chirping of spring and building their nests for the future. A heady optimism filled me, erasing any fear of illness as I tossed peanuts at the eager sparrows.

I was set for life. I could come in at nine-thirty and leave at four and make a fortune. Fifty million more under management! That's seventy million in all, plenty to make a living off without scalping anyone.

A large crow landed at my feet and hopped around, scooping up peanuts. When he got a little too close, I threw the peanuts six feet away from me. Still he kept moving towards me with his giant beak open so I threw the bag on the ground and he grabbed it and flew away.

The crow is the bird of Apollo because they're so smart. What about Apollo? And poetry?

I had been worshipping Hermes for so long that all I cared about was money. But once there's money, what else is there to care about? The manic energy of my job was anathema to the 'dropping slow' observations that comprise a poem. Had numbers and prices extinguished my imagination?

My life had become so filled with the daily run of business that I didn't reflect anymore on the big questions. Perhaps that was a good thing. Perhaps it was good to leave Apollo and his love of meaning behind.

But what about mortality? Looking up at the bright day, I saw the summer green leaves swaying in the breeze. Soon they would be falling.

I found myself at the end of an allee of tulips planted in memory of those who died of AIDS. I reached up and felt the gland on my neck and shook my head. Nonsense! Ate had me firmly in her spell of blindness.

I sat down on a green bench in front of a cloud of red tulips dedicated to the dead.

On the bench opposite me was a handsome, older businessman with green eyes. He was staring at me in the provocative way of gay men and I stared back with recognition. He touched himself beneath his newspaper within my view. I got up and sat beside him on the bench.

"You got a place?"

"No."

"How's the stairwell in your building?"

This didn't sound like a good idea, but Aphrodite was urging me on. As we started walking out of the park, a squirrel came up and scolded me as they are wont to do. Only later would I realize that it was Athena, my better judgment, warning me about what I was doing. I chuckled quizzically at the small creature and kept walking.

We took the elevator of my building to a floor one flight below the ones occupied by the firm and slipped into the stairwell unnoticed. But in the middle of the act, the door above us opened and the voices of Wolf and Gluck crashed into the silence like a panic. They heard us shuffling our clothes on.

"Who's down there?" shouted Wolf, peering over the edge.

My heart leaped to my throat. I scurried down the stairs, clinging to the outside walls as they craned their necks to see the intruders, shouting angrily now. Twenty flights down we exited at a lower floor and pressed the elevator buttons. I didn't want to exit at the lobby in case they called down there. The stranger took an elevator downstairs and I went back up to the office, covered in sweat.

I couldn't believe I was acting so compulsively at work again, risking everything. No city ordinance in the world would protect me from a charge of lewdness at the office.

I was wiping my brow as Gluck came by.

"Where the hell have you been?" he demanded.

"I took a long walk to digest the new situation," I improvised. "It's hot out there," I added to account for the sweaty brow.

"This is the wrong signal to send me about how you're going to handle this partnership," he scolded me. "I told her to work with Wolf or Rose but she insisted on you. Now don't prove me right. Lunch is the best part of the day so this better not become a habit."

He stormed off and left me with a guilty face and a sweaty brow. I kept imagining the scene I barely escaped.

"Don't even clean out your desk," Gluck would have said, "Just get out."

Big Nose was staring at me.

"What's the matter with you?"

I told him about Jill.

"You're a lucky stiff," he said, genuinely pleased for me. "Play your cards right and you'll get the whole ball of wax."

"Yes," I said, shaking off my nerves and trying to act as cool as Athena, the god I had spurned.

"You know why she chose you?" he said. "Because you were on the verge of tears in that meeting. She thinks you're a sensitive guy she can control. So don't go feeling overly grateful. She's acting in her own interest, setting herself up to collect half your income and show up only once a week. Let's just hope she goes with her father and makes a clean break. Then you'll be the master of Gluck instead of his slave. You'll be able to take that money to some other firm and he'll know it. So congratulations, you practically got it made."

"You're a lucky fucking asshole," said Rose, her eyes gleaming with envy.

"I'll take being lucky over getting what I deserve."

Just how lucky became apparent when I started making the calls. These investors had never really been sold to before.

"What are you buying today?" asked one business owner.

"Mercury Systems," I told him and gave him my pitch.

"Buy me two thousand shares," he said and hung up.

The phone rang a moment later.

"What was that stock again?"

Jill was surprised at how quickly I built large positions in the accounts. We soon had thousands of shares in IBM, Pepsi, GE, Mercury Systems, and Colgate.

"I can't believe we have 20,000 shares of Pepsi," she said covering her mouth. "I was never good at building positions. I was too afraid."

"We buy the same stocks for everyone," I told her, "so we can sell them all at the same time and move into something else."

"When do we sell?" she asked.

"When they run out of money for new ideas."

She smiled, taken aback at how easily I was re-shaping her business.

"Of course, there can be other reasons to sell," I told her.

"What are those reasons?"

"When we need the money."

"Yes," she said, "I have plenty of bills to pay," as she clutched the pearl necklace hanging down her neck in her fingers.

The Slayer of Argus

Over the next few weeks, I bought fifty thousand shares of Mercury Systems in her accounts. It was like taking candy from a baby. I came in early and left late and never got off the phone. Gluck was tickled pink. I ran in to Father Zeus to show him the buy ticket for the fifty thousandth share.

"You have done a fine job working your accounts," he said.

"You mean Jill's accounts,"

"No, I mean your accounts," he said adamantly. "Jill gave up those accounts and she never put them in stocks because she couldn't face people with a loss. All that money in Limited Partnerships is dead until the Second Coming. You should liquidate them and take the losses and get that money moving again."

"Jill calls them a core holding."

"There's no such thing as a 'core holding'," he fumed. "It's a buy or a sell if you want to be successful in this business. And why are you still at that old desk? You should be in the empty office."

"That's Jill's office. Shouldn't you discuss this with her first?"

"I did."

I believed the rumor of Jill's affair with Gluck but he sure wasn't acting like a lover now. Of course, it could be that he loved commissions more than he loved any woman. But every Friday when she came in they left together after market.

And so I moved into the glass periphery away from the rookies in the middle of the room. Big Nose helped me turn my desk around to face the Harbor with Governor's Island floating below me and put my back to the boss, which no one else dared to do. Then I moved her *Ficus* between the desk and the glass wall so I'd be out of the boss' line of sight.

"Nice knowin ya," said Big Nose.

I emptied the desk and boxed her files, then took down her posters and replaced them with my own, including a large print of the Hermes by Praxiteles. As the final ritual touch, I got a fishbowl with a goldfish named Pepsi, and put Peter Pan behind the bowl so I could see him through the water.

"Don't die, Pepsi," I begged it. "I'll lose too many accounts if you float belly up."

I felt like a fine gentleman in a painting by Titian. I worked hard and never worried whether Gluck was watching me or not. When he passed by, I didn't get off the phone calls with friends, because I was producing.

Jill showed up on Friday.

The quizzical look on her face and the sudden heaving of her chest told me that Gluck had not spoken with her about taking her desk.

"What the hell is going on here?"

"Jill, I…"

"What the hell is going on here?" she shouted, drawing all eyes to us. I felt like Odysseus giving Circe the brush.

Gluck appeared at the door.

"Come into my office."

She sobbed on his shoulder on the couch in his corner office. When they emerged, she clung calmly to his arm and there was a mound lengthening down his pants leg.

Her hair was wet when they came back from lunch. I got up to cede her the chair but she stopped me saying, "No, it's your desk. It's silly for me to have it when I'm only in once a week. But we are still equal partners. It's a little sad, that's all."

She was a friend of Aphrodite and Hermes, gods of pleasure who like nice things. Her musical voice soothed the customers with talk of guarantees and maturities, but there was also a voracious Siren behind it all, eager to pick over their bones.

"I do like the way you turned the desk around," she said in that musical voice, "Such a lovely view I wasted all those years, and it's nice having the fig tree positioned for privacy."

Her visits became fewer and shorter as she got more deeply involved with her father's business. Always she complained about her sister, who didn't want her horning in on the business and opposed her every investment decision.

"She resents my being there," she said, "but it's my right and I'm my father's daughter, too. It's just frustrating. They're real traders, those two."

"How do they manage the money?"

"They go in and out of Fidelity accounts at the end of the day, trying to time the market and pick the right sectors. Pretty simple, huh?"

"That's a money manager?" I asked, amazed at the simple gimmick.

I knew I couldn't trust Jill so I decided to follow Gluck's advice and sell out the Limited Partnerships at a loss so the clients would turn against her. That was Athena's treacherous strategy in service to Hermes' greed.

The blood ran in the streets. The clients cursed Jill and I didn't contradict them when they said she screwed them.

"She just isn't comfortable with the fluctuation of stocks," I said in halfhearted defense. I could be a Siren as well.

When Jill saw the trades she despaired.

"How am I ever going to face those people?"

"I'll handle them for you."

That money went into GE, Exxon, and Pepsi. As the months went by, clients stopped asking about Jill and several of them told me they'd follow me if I left the firm.

"How is the partnership going?" she'd ask, and I'd grimace like an indentured servant.

"Don't sell anything else without my permission," she said sternly.

"We need to clean up these portfolios."

She was a bird of prey, her tiny dark eyes shrinking around her beak of a nose as she looked over the trades with incredulity.

"You sold out the Marotta's?" she cringed. "I promised them they couldn't lose. They can't lose. If you meet them, you'll understand. I know it sounds mean but they're pigs: fat and low class from deepest darkest Brooklyn. They have disgusting appetites and no culture, even though they're Italian like me."

"Lulu has a beautiful deep voice."

"She's a pig, too. And I'm telling you they cannot lose money. These are the kind of people who boast about being connected, if you know what I mean. They might have me thrown in the river."

"With concrete shoes?" I laughed. "Every Italian in Providence claims he's connected, too."

She sighed and sat down.

"Lulu was a walk-in," she explained, "She showed up one day with a grocery bag with three hundred thousand dollars in it. I told her I couldn't deposit cash, but she told me to figure it out. It was supposedly a settlement from the union for her husband, who got 'injured on the job', as she put it. But God knows what he really did for that money. So I took the bag home. Naturally, it was a rainy day and there were no cabs and the bag was getting wet, so I had to take the loot onto the subway. You can imagine how it felt, being crowded with people with a wet paper bag about to fall apart with three hundred thousand dollars in it and thinking that everyone knew what was going on."

"I know that feeling," I said, not knowing that the gods were about to make me feel it again.

Jill got distracted by her father's illness and didn't come in for a month.

"How are his spirits?"

"He's taking it so well," she said, catching her breath. "He says he's had a good life and that he has three beautiful daughters," and then she broke down, choking.

He died on Thanksgiving surrounded by his family on a cot in the living room. He didn't know who he was or what was happening.

There was a throng of limousines at the funeral. The room was piled high with flowers. The three beautiful, dark sisters stood by the coffin looking like the Three Graces dressed in black, weeping on each other's shoulder and holding their tiny old mother in the dance of grief.

"I won't be in for a while," Jill said.

I was glad to be alone again.

I started shopping for an apartment in Chelsea, which was becoming the 'gay suburbs' for refugees from the Village and its high rents.

The day before my closing, Jill came in with a sheepish grin.

"I'm back."

"Back what?"

"I'm back full time. I can't stand my sister. The bitch has driven me out. Let her have the damn business. I can't work with her, it would break up the family."

"You're coming in every day now?"

"Well that's what I want to talk to you about, Michael," she said, readying to cast her whammy. "Either you let me become your full time partner, sharing all your accounts with me, or I will dissolve the partnership. Gluck's behind me on this."

"That wasn't the agreement," I stammered.

"There is nothing in writing. If you don't agree to share your commissions I'll simply take back my accounts."

She folded her arms.

I went in to speak with Gluck.

"You said she couldn't come back."

"She's back."

I called the Legal Department. They assured me that a manager could do whatever he wants and that I couldn't move to another office either.

I took Jill's terms.

"I'm glad you understand," she said in that deep, relaxed voice, her powers fully restored as she touched up her lipstick. "I would have gone it alone if I had to," she said smiling.

Gluck took us both out to lunch.

"Let's make it a real partnership," he said. "If Jill ever leaves, you get it all, no strings. You're lucky," he assured me with a pat on the back.

"Just a little less lucky than yesterday," laughed Jill, jabbing her fork into a piece of chocolate cake.

We managed to squeeze a second desk into the glass office. My every pitch and advice was analyzed and vetted. I showed Jill every ticket with the joint commission number on it.

"Good work," she'd say or, "Ease up on them. I don't want you churning."

She listened to my personal calls as well, responding to everything I said with no pretense at privacy. I told my friends that the word 'travel' meant I couldn't speak freely.

She sold bonds while I sold stocks. She took on her version of a Zeus voice when she called them up, sounding so serious and professional in a grown up voice quite different from her normal speaking voice as she outlined the ratings, coupons and maturity of the various bonds she was peddling. She made it all sound so important, trying to make a story out of every little tenth of a percent.

Sometimes she would shrug her shoulders and say, "It is what it is," as though stating a religious mystery. "It's three percent tax free and with this rating there's little risk."

She was not a born salesman. She sounded unnatural. She seemed to hide behind the sales persona, confusing herself with it, as though she was masking her true feelings. But I made no comment.

The workday was like an endless sales meeting. Circe had me trapped with her shared commission and her gassy snacks and now I couldn't escape because I had a mortgage to pay.

But the Fates came to my rescue with the New Year when it turned out that Jill's commissions, cut over the last year from our period of sharing, didn't meet the bogey for normal payout, meaning that her income was reduced by two thirds. I heard her talking low on the phone and ending calls when I walked into the room, so I knew some new god was afoot.

Meanwhile Big Nose confronted me in the locker room about a purple mark on the back of my arm not covered by my t-shirt.

"This looks like the same thing I saw on the back of your calf," he said. "Are those other marks still there?"

With one sweep he bent down and pulled up the leg of my sweatpants.

"Jesus Christ," he said. The calf was covered. He pointed out several others I hadn't seen.

I pulled down the leg and smirked. He insisted I get it checked out.

"It's probably nothing but it could be serious," he said, trying to convince me by softening the sale and adding a little threat like he did with the insurance clients.

Jill overheard our hushed conversations.

"Michael, are you concerned about your health?"

"I'm fine," I insisted. We were both Hermes trying to deceive each other in that small space.

"No matter what happens," she said in a mothering voice, "I will be one hundred percent behind you."

With a knife, I said to myself.

....

I read the warning signs of melanoma in the waiting room of the skin doctor, Dr. Faust, whose name terrified me.

"Are you gay, Michael?" he asked. I knew I wasn't feminine.

"Why do you ask?"

"These lesions look like Kaposi's Sarcoma."

"No!"

"It's a good chance it's K.S."

"How much of a chance?"

"Ten percent, say."

"Ten percent." I jumped on that. "I can beat those odds."

"Well maybe twenty percent," said the doctor. He lowered the lamp over the metallic table I was laying on in my underwear to examine more closely. The office was chilly under that fluorescent light.

"Look," he said, pointing mercilessly like Medusa at the twenty odd lesions melding together among the scrapes on my right ankle and another dozen scattered on my thighs and arms. He pushed the bright fluorescent light over the worst part of the ankle and I felt Ate's blindness burning off like fog.

"I'm writing 'picker's nodules' on the diagnosis for now. Show me one that's most recent."

"You think it's picker's nodules?" I asked anxiously, pointing out a bright spot that appeared recently.

"Let's say forty percent chance it's K.S."

"Those odds keep going up," I protested.

He smiled as he sliced off the mark with a scalpel and sent me home with instructions to call in a week for the results.

"Forty percent chance," I said to Big Nose, who nodded thoughtfully.

I couldn't sleep waiting for the results because my heart knew the truth. When I called the doctor, the lab hadn't reported back yet.

"Bad news travels fast," said Big Nose reassuringly. "You look as healthy as an ox. You should be in competition. Just look at you. If it was AIDS, they'd have called already."

I prepared my father.

"AIDS," he said, his voice quavering. "That makes no sense."

"I just want you to know that the doctor said it was a possibility."

No one mentioned my sexuality, not Big Nose, not my father. That god was *in the room* as the Greeks would say, and no one cared.

The next day the tests were in. The nurse refused to give me the results.

"Bad news travels quickly," I told her. She put on the doctor.

"How are you?" he asked in a busy voice.

"That's why I'm calling."

"It's been lovely weather since I saw you."

"What's the story?"

"You're in good shape," he said. "But yes, it's Kaposi's Sarcoma. I knew that when I saw you. I just had to get the biopsy because there was so much denial."

"I've got AIDS?" I asked, hearing my voice from miles away.

"Yes."

My chest started heaving. I closed my eyes tightly.

"How long do I have?"

"Now that we have AZT," he said, mulling, "maybe two years. But then there might be more drugs, so if you can surf ahead of the wave of new drugs you can live indefinitely."

When I opened my eyes I saw Jill leaning against the partition behind the *Ficus* with her hand on her mouth.

"It's really AIDS?" she asked, amazed as she followed me to the elevator. I was heading home, dizzy with the news. "You've got AIDS?" she kept repeating like a harpy and searching my face.

"Yes, I have AIDS," I relented. "The three ugliest words in the English language."

"Oh Michael," she moaned. "You've just thrown a wrench in my plans. On Friday, I was going to tell you I was leaving the business to go work in the bond department, but now I don't know what to do."

Quickly I realized how foolish I was to tell her anything. If she left the business, my salary would double overnight and I'd have enough money to make the most of whatever life was left.

"I'll be fine," I assured her, gripping control of myself and not daring to think. "People live longer and longer with AZT. I've got to go now."

She rode down the elevator with me like a sympathizing Argus, staring at me and scrutinizing me with a hundred eyes.

"You really have AIDS," she kept saying, "You really have AIDS," her wings beating behind her as she beheld her prey, her face taking on a strange beauty.

Out on the sunny street, my head swam with realization. The sounds of traffic were heightened, as were the frail colors of the approaching twilight. That which I most feared had come to pass and I felt strangely free, untethered to the earth like a helium balloon let go and falling into the sky. Everything around me seemed alive and the streets swarmed with people, even though it was a normal, quiet afternoon.

I called my mother.

"It's bad."

She was already weeping when she put my father on the phone. He and I had finally found refuge for a friendship talking about the stock market. I had changed in his eyes from a scornful elitist to a savvy stockbroker living in the big city, and he preferred Hermes to Apollo. In return for his silence on the subject, I kept my boyfriends away from home.

He choked and coughed on the phone, struggling against himself. I had never heard my father weep before.

When I put the phone down I went to the video store and rented the 'Three Stooges' and 'I love Lucy' and headed back up the Avenue, hoping that Zeus' harsh reality could be tempered by some of Hermes' comedy. Dusty got a lot of treats leaning against me on the couch.

Now Ate, the goddess of my blindness, was gone. The voices denying my illness were vanquished. It had all been said and to people who mattered to me. 'I have AIDS' kept running through my head, and the only drug available was surrounded by doubts and controversy.

As I stood on the street corner waiting for the light, I was amazed at the nearness of everything. The sound of the bus driving by was louder than before. The smell of the pavement drying after the quick rain was musty and permeating. "I have AIDS," I told myself, "But I am here right now."

I kept expecting the ground to open up and swallow me in broad daylight. It was a magnificent, summer day and I felt like a shadow from the Underworld, visiting the world of the living in my bubble of darkness. Everything seemed hyper-real and at the same time like a dream.

Big Nose and Rose showed up later that evening with wine and cheese. We snacked and talked and I cried on Rose's shoulder. They left late and my grief and the wine put me to sleep.

I dreamt about a giant cave full of ancestors, like giant heads standing around the bed watching me under the covers. They knew. In Hades, all the secrets come out. I saw my future self, wearing a blackish purple plate of cancer like an exoskeleton, thin with the starvation of the dying, tended by a loyal few whose patience sees me off kindly at the end.

Hermes was leading me down as *Psychopompos,* the Guide of Souls. Naively, willfully, I had clung to Herakles the Hero, who defies the limits imposed by the gods and believes in the inevitable march of progress and that my life was 'mine' to begin with, a matter between me and the gods. The money going up and up seemed to prove it all until suddenly the Thief in the Night swindled me out of my blindness, like Jack felling the Giant.

Hermes was in charge all along. The god who leads the dying souls down to his friend, Hades, had been waiting patiently during my years of denial, content in his knowledge like a bondholder watching a due date. I had turned my back on Apollo and writing and scraped the marks of mortality from my body and this was the payback, this sudden plunge into the always-shocking fact of death, for which no amount of resignation or serenity can prepare anyone.

Now I was falling backwards in the dark. I had tried to become Hermes on my own terms, but it is the gods who set the terms of friendship. I woke up at three in a sweat and shivered with Dusty stretched out with his back against me. We slept on a towel.

Now I had to figure out how to handle Jill. How could I deny what I had just told her? I had to lull her to sleep by being brave and hopeful, minimizing my illness and stressing the new drug, AZT, in order to slay the beast for good.

I put on my best blue suit, a crisp shirt, and a new red tie. I shone my shoes and touched a little base makeup under my eyes to hide the swelling. In the tiny mirror that now graced my altar, I caught my blue eyes and ritually dressed myself in Hermes' easy smile and cheerful face.

"Help me out," I implored the image, preparing for my toughest sales job ever. For good luck, I stuffed the little broken statue of Peter Pan into my pocket and put on the metal cock ring.

I crammed into the subway wondering who else had AIDS. There were fifty people in the car. Surely someone else was harboring this secret. Were they wondering the same thing? Did they all know about me? At every station, people streamed on and off in their chaotic tangents of destination.

Usually a late bird, Jill was already in her chair and on the phone when I arrived. She got off the phone immediately and swiveled around to look at me, all smiles and concern, her hundred eyes turned upon my face, scrutinizing. On the desk stood an enormous bouquet of white tulips in a glass vase.

I thanked her, shuddering, and took them out of the glass vase to remove the rubber band. They lounged now in the glass, their necks hanging over the rim.

"So how are you?" she asked, singing the 'are' in that lovely, deep voice, throwing nets of concern around me. She was a giant bird, ready to peck at my body.

"So much better," I said, feigning relief. "It's not as bad as it sounded yesterday. It's not the end of the world after all. My bloods are very high and the doctor feels I'm steady. I've had skin problems my whole life so there's nothing new, really. Lots of Syrians get this anyway, so it may just be genetic. Of all the symptoms I could get, this is the least serious. Jill, I'll be fine."

"Would you ever consider leaving the business?" she asked, cutting through my distraction.

"Never," I parried. "I love this business. I am here to stay. I'm healthy enough except for some skin rashes. In fact, this doesn't even constitute a real diagnosis. It simply means I'm positive," I lied, counting on her ignorance.

We looked each other in the eyes and I tried not to open mine too widely. She was a grimacing Medusa.

"This business is what I was made for," I said, "It's what I really want to do with my life. It gives me meaning and I will never leave. What about you? You were telling me only yesterday…"

"I had a job lined up, Michael, but now I'd like to have a while to think it over. You really feel that confident that you're up to this? I'd hate for something to happen to you in a year and the accounts go to someone else. Maybe I should stay and inherit your accounts instead of you inheriting mine."

"I'm the same as I've been for the last five years," I told her. "I've had these marks all along. A lot of people are positive and don't ever get sick. I'll be fine."

I kept thinking, 'sleep, Argus, sleep', the way Hermes lulled the monster with the hundred eyes to sleep over wine and conversation before he slew him by cutting them all off at once.

"You're inspiring, Michael," she said sighing. "My father was inspiring too. He was so brave and he never complained. He looked good right up to the end. You would never have known. Have you had a good life, Michael?"

I winced.

"A great one so far, and I'm not going anywhere soon," I sang. "Just look at me." I flexed a bicep through my suit jacket. "You have no idea how common this condition is, a kind of pre-AIDS that can continue forever, now that they have AZT."

"That's supposed to be working, isn't it?" she asked, unsure.

"And there are new drugs coming down the pipeline," I assured her. "I just got freaked out yesterday, you know, finding out I'm positive. But there's a lot of things I can do to keep it from progressing, so it may never develop into full-blown AIDS."

Lull-a-bye and goodnight, the angels will guide you, lull-a-bye and goodnight, the boogeyman will eat you. I waited for the spell to work.

"What about the skin cancer?" she asked, looking right and left. "Isn't that serious?"

"You know skin cancer is the most easily cured cancer, darling," I reminded her, glossing over the fact that it meant an AIDS diagnosis. "When they get rid of the lesion, I'll just be positive again, not even ARC, which is the pre-AIDS I was talking about."

"But when you left yesterday, Michael, you said you had AIDS."

"That was before I met with the doctor," I lied. "I was just a little shocked, as you can imagine. You know how I tend to dramatize," I said, camping it up.

The hundred eyes were drooping now. I didn't even dare to think the truth, because they would detect my fear and open again.

"I was feeling sorry for myself," I said, as though coaxing an old friend, "I'm a big baby and you see what a perfectionist I am with this mania for the gym. Lots of Syrians get this skin condition anyway, and I might not even be positive. My uncle had something like this and he lived into his nineties."

Tell them once. Tell them twice.

"Did you get the test?"

"Everyone should get the test," I said like Athena the Concerned Citizen. "It was the rash that bothered me," suppressing the word 'lesion', "so I'm going to get rid of it."

Only two or three of the eyes were still watchful, floating on their tentacles. The others were closed and asleep. The spell was working.

"Another common side effect," avoiding the word, 'symptom', "is dandruff and dry skin. Thank God I don't have that yet, because I hate that medicated shampoo smell. Don't you?"

I was eager to enlist other senses in the distraction.

"What is it, Selsun Blue?" I chuckled, "a pungent, minty smell."

"I have dandruff," she said, the last lids drooping, "I think you've been pretending you didn't notice," and then all the eyes were shut.

I had noticed. I needed her to identify with health issues instead of pinning all those gods on me.

I repeated the story several times to various friends in a low voice meant to be eavesdropped, and she didn't disappoint me. Of course, I was talking to Big Nose over and over again, but she didn't know that. *Tell them once, tell them twice.*

For the next two weeks, my stance became more upright and my mien more chipper. At home, I would collapse and grieve.

"Next week will be my last week here, Michael," she informed me one morning. "I'm going to Greece for three glorious weeks with a girlfriend of mine and then I'm starting my new job."

"Greece!" I shouted, attributing my visible glee to her upcoming trip. "I've been there once and I would kill to go back. Three weeks! That's a real journey, not just a trip."

"Now we've got to convince Gluck that you're capable of handling the partnership alone."

"I've handled it fine all along."

"That was before we knew you were sick. Michael, your health is a question mark and I probably shouldn't be leaving you right now."

"I'm fine. You can see I'm fine. Right now, what's important is your happiness and you're taking charge of that like a pro."

She paused.

"If Gluck finds out he'll make you take on another partner and then we're both screwed. He might even ask me to come back. So keep it a secret."

"I wasn't planning on telling him. He could make me take on a new partner?"

"What do you think?" she asked me triumphantly.

"Mum's the word."

"I certainly don't want to tell him, but I do feel a little funny not telling him, if you know what I mean. I have a responsibility to my clients to see that they wind up in good hands."

"Please don't tell him," I said, trying to sound confident but I could hear my voice pleading. "I don't want another partner. No one could take your place as my partner. This really has been fun."

"I'm leaving you with a real business, Michael," she said, weighing her words. "You should kiss the ground I walk on. Don't you think I deserve more than a handshake? I certainly don't want to tell Gluck about your condition, but that should be worth something, too, for I have to live with that secret."

"What are we talking about?"

"Thirty-five percent of your salary in cash for two years and I won't breathe a word," she said, her dulcet voice ringing in my ears like an echo chamber. "And I want the monthly commission run to prove you're trading in our number, not your own--although of course I trust you, that's not the question. This is just business."

I was silent. The room was crashing down around me.

"Call it a residual commission, or a trailer," she explained. ""I've built this business from the ground up and you should buy it from me. It's a great investment for you and it's only for two years. Gluck will never need to know anything. It's a win-win for everyone."

She smiled and held out her hand. I shook it, squeezing my hand firmly around hers as a last show of strength, but I was a ghost in a suit.

Two years was all I had left, according to the doctor. It was blackmail, not an investment, no matter how she wantod to paint it.

Gluck called me into his office.

"Congratulations," he said, shaking my hand. "Your cold-calling days are over. Now go do four hundred for me."

Four hundred thousand in commissions was pie in the sky but I let it go.

"'Your cold-calling days are over,'" repeated Big Nose after Market. "I wish I could have seen Gluck's face when he said that. Remember how he screwed you with Becker? And how he screwed you when Jill came back? Now he can't touch you."

He put his foot up on his desk.

"One thing you ought to do," he said, "is throw Jill a going away party to make it official."

"The ritual will make it harder for her to come back," I mused, comprehending.

I set about ordering champagne, arranging a cake, and buying a fine Teddy Bear made in Germany with Jill's name stitched on its heart. When her last day came, I festooned the conference room with white crepe paper and put several vases of white tulips on the giant table as my own little jab from the Underworld.

Jill cried when she saw the tulips. I led the men in a round of 'For She's a Jolly Good Fellow' for a classy touch and she was genuinely flattered.

Before she left, I looked at her desk and saw a list of the major clients and their phone numbers.

"That's my safety net, Michael," she said, walking in as I pored over it. "In case something happens, you know."

She looked at the river glistening in the autumn sun.

"One word of advice, Michael. Go meet the clients. Take them to dinner, to coffee, or have them into the office. Spend some time with them and become a part of their lives. God knows I could never pick a stock for beans but I made them feel like family so they'd feel guilty leaving me. That's what you should do."

I frowned as we said goodbye. I knew she saw it.

"See you next month with the loot," she smirked.

Back home, as I sat in a comfortable chair, a strange feeling gripped me, a kind of non-recognition. My name, the events of my life, the people who loved me, were all as if set aside as I peered at the wall and forgot who I was. I was back in the dentist's chair, witnessing my life from the outside like

Hekate, the witch goddess, the one who lives in a cave by the entrance to Hades, the one who witnessed the rape of Persephone and said nothing. Disasters don't surprise her. She expects nothing less than disaster from life.

That night, I dreamt I was at the old house where I grew up and I found a door behind the dresser that led through a series of rooms that became increasingly oddly shaped, until they became triangles and the doors banged into each other and it was impossible to continue. I stood before a pile of treasure like a dragon's horde, gleaming gold, silver, emeralds, rubies, and diamonds and piles of ancient jewelry. I gathered up as many gems and coins I could in my stretched out sweatshirt. And then I saw my Syrian grandmother standing and watching me with her arms folded. The smile she made was obscene.

When I awoke, it was four in the morning and I was hard.

That erection kept me awake and only went soft in rebellion when I tried to quell it on my own. As soon as I tried to sleep again, it came back. Eros wants sex when death feels near.

I threw on my jeans and headed over to the baths. At that hour, the booth store was closed and any men determined to score that night were already inside or on the line that stretched down the stairway to the basement of the run-down Deco building on Twentieth Street.

Some of them wore fine clothes, having been to theater or dinner hours earlier wearing another persona with friends who had already gone to sleep. Others wore leather or jeans. They all had a dazed look as they leaned against the bannister, keeping their eyes away from one another like figures on a Greek vase. Up the stairs came an employee of the establishment, a fresh looking Puerto Rican in a tight white t-shirt and jeans carrying a flashlight and a bag that smelled of coffee.

"There's plenty of space in the waiting room," he announced in a chipper voice colored by the Spanish *l* and *s*. "Please move along," he beckoned, waving the flashlight.

The herd of men trudged down the dark stairs, gibbering among themselves. Some leaned on others, drunk or stoned, following the kindly guide. They made little flitting gestures like bats as they held each other in place, their faces devoid of expression. The shower area was visible through an opaque glass wall along the black painted lobby and the black tile floor with a large white couch looming towards the counter. An enormous and grandiose display of orchids and birds-of-paradise stood guard by the entrance like strange flowers of the Underworld under a photo of forget-me-nots in the snow.

Inside I felt as though I was still dreaming as I passed men in towels pacing through the passageways. My feet moved automatically as I fell into the flow, peeking compulsively into the tiny rooms at the various scenes of indulgence.

I felt completely invisible. It was dark in that labyrinth so at least they couldn't see my marks. Finally I went in with someone.

....

A month later Jill called.

"Meet me at the entrance to the Winter Garden and put it in a paper bag, please," she said in her professional, grown up bond-selling Zeus voice.

I asked Big Nose to come with me to ease the meeting. Jill showed up with another woman her age.

"We are traveling together," she told us, introducing her friend, who was in her fifties.

I handed her the paper bag.

"Is this the loot?" she asked smiling, "So how's the partnership?"

"Business is good. I put all the calculations in the bag."

"So how are you?" she sang. "Are you taking good care of yourself?"

"I feel great."

They left, Jill's friend leaning on her as though her feet ached.

"These wounded women kill me," said Big Nose. "Hardworking, middle-aged, tragic. All her friends have this crippled look. And what's this bullshit about a partnership? She's out."

"I thought you liked women who'd lost hope."

When I got back to the office, there was a message from Jill.

"You're cheating me," she announced. "I want a copy of the commission run."

I had sliced off one percent, so we arranged a time to meet again with the extra few hundred dollars. We both went with our bodyguards and this time there was no flirting or smiles.

The next month, I saved all the syndicate business until the last day of commission so it wouldn't show up on the daily run I gave her. I was able to hide twenty percent of the take, which was my revenge for her blackmail. Hermes always gets even.

This time when we met, the women were tan from their trip.

"We got robbed," said Jill, "I don't want to talk about Greece."

"Any Greek lovers?" asked Big Nose. "Didja take it up the back door?"

They smiled awkwardly and left us in the palm court.

"She's no partner, my friend," said Big Nose. "She's your enemy. I don't know why she has this power over you, but you have to take her on. You have to go meet the clients and make them yours so you can cut her bawls off."

Among the Shades

"Michael, we've got to have you for dinner."

Lulu Marotta's dulcet voice rang over the phone so melodiously that I asked her if she was a singer.

"You're a charmer," she said. "Ever since you got rid of that bitch Jill who stuck me in that piece of shit America First, we've thought nothing but good about you, Michael. We love you, Michael. Come on Sunday and bring someone if you can. We don't care if it's a guy or a girl. We'll take you as you are. Tell me, Michael, are you gay?"

"Lulu," I gasped, "You're amazing." She was no stranger to Hermes either, for she obviously knew how to flatter. This was tho matriarch of the 'family of pigs' Jill told me about.

"I'm just whoring around still," I told her, to match her directness.

Her rippling laugh of pleasure pulled me in.

"I love that you can be yourself with me," she said. And then her tone got serious. "You are being careful out there, aren't you? You're watching out for that AIDS I hope."

"I've had my wild days," I told her, hedging.

"Michael, we don't care who does what with who," she assured me. "Fuck, suck, it's all the same to us as long as you're getting some if you want it. I tell you, my Ed's getting old. We had out anniversary, forty three years."

"Congratulations. How wonderful."

"Forty three years with the same goddamned dick," she moaned. "Can you imagine how awful? He thinks he's a stud in bed and of course, I have no basis of comparison. When I got married I hadn't been with anyone else. I just lie there, waiting for something to happen, but I mostly get a bellyache with him huffing and puffing on top of me. And he's as fat as me so it ain't logistical and it ain't pretty to look at. So while he's plugging away I just try to think about what I'm going to cook for supper—about anything else but what's happening and wait till he's done."

Then she sounded almost angry, the years of Hera's spousal loyalty having worn down Aphrodite's patience.

"He expects me to go down on him but would he ever go down on me?" she said, outraged. "I see on T.V. the stuff the hot young things are doing and I say, hell, I can do that. I want to go out Michael, when my Ed finally goes"—and this she said with a sigh of anticipated grief—"and it's going to be one of these years soon because of his hypertension. I'm going to go out and really live it up because you only live once. I'm going to fuck, I'm going to suck, and I'm going to do everyone and everything before it's too late. Can you blame me, Michael?"

I was holding my breath.

"Can you blame me?" she insisted, then, "We love you, Michael," she repeated, fawning over me, the lovely bell tone of her voice sounding clear through the wire. "Now, I don't want you to be surprised, but I just want you to know that we're a little big here."

She considered a moment.

"We're a lot big, on the fatter side. We have good hearts though, we Marottas. We don't judge people. 'Stare lascia stare' we say. We want to welcome you into the family."

I took the subway out to Greenpoint which was at that time the heart of white lower middle class Brooklyn where warehouses alternated with big plain, square houses in a landscape devoid of ornament or trees. Tina's house was a plain concrete block with a large cement container of plastic ivy chained to the front stoop.

"There you are honey," said a shadow looming behind the screen door. It was the beautiful voice from the phone.

"Give us a kiss, we meet at last."

The door opened and she moved backwards to make room in the narrow hallway. Lulu was enormous in her yellow-green stretch poly sweats big enough to sail a small boat. She held out her hand, which stretched out of an arm slim from the elbow down with huge billows of fat hanging above it as like floodwaters held back by a dam.

"Both cheeks," I insisted as we pecked at each other.

The eight people in the room weighed as much as twenty normal people. The dining set was giant size with chairs as big as love seats.

"Look how handsome he is," said the enormous dyed blond who showed me my seat.

"Meet Tommy," said Lulu. "Our neighbor. He owns the funeral parlor next door. You must have seen it coming down the avenue."

I shook hands with the old bachelor, who had a trim Satanic look with a moustache and Van Dyke. When he spoke, I recognized Apollo's gay tones and exaggerated enunciation.

They treated him like Zeus. Everyone was silent whenever he spoke in his sharp, deep voice and emphatic manner, even when he was talking to just one of them. He was reserved towards me, playing Apollo's game of pretending not to notice we were both gay.

"Lulu makes the best antipasto in Brooklyn," he announced to the room.

"I can't compete with Bastante's," she confessed. "They've got male chefs and male waiters, even cloth napkins. Very fancy." With this, her enormous body did a girlish cursty to dramatize the elegance of the place.

This conversation had obviously been rehearsed so many times it had become a ritual among them. I counted on hearing many such ritual speeches that evening.

"Tommy took me and the family last month for New Year's," she continued, holding up her head proudly as if wearing a crown. "He's a real sport and he takes good care of us. It's been so hard for him lately. How many deaths are you dealing with, Tommy?"

"Twelve in the last month."

"I'm so sorry," I said in horror. "Relative or friends?"

"Customers," he answered, "It's the nature of the business. I dress them all, prepare them, and help the families through the tough parts. Who wants to decide about lasagna or cutlets when someone just died? Why burn the guy's best suit if it fits his son perfectly fine? And there's always the conundrum about burying the ring. But one really got to me: remember Billy Cola?" he called to Lulu, who nodded obediently. We were in ritual land again.

"I knew him thirty-two years. He used to run the paper route here. Dead at thirty-two. That's obscene," he declared, sitting up tall. "I'm seventy and I think people should not be dying at thirty-two."

"Was it what we all think it was?" asked Lulu, putting her hands over her ears.

Tommy didn't answer.

"I nursed him through the last months. There was no charge for the funeral. I did it out of love. He was a good boy, full of promise. I don't give a shit what he did in bed. We were always friends. His family treated him like shit though. They were ashamed of his illness and tried to keep it a secret. And it's too bad. It's just an illness, no meaning to it at all. Yeah, I've seen a lot of death in my day."

He laughed a quick, painful laugh that crackled into a cough that went on for a minute and left him sputtering for breath. Then he lit a cigar.

"Is everyone here Catholic?" I ventured.

"Fallen Catholics," said Tommy. "The Pope says this and then he says that. Every time they change the rules the host of souls moves up or down the elevator from Purgatory to Hell. I know inside what Jesus meant so I go with that. He didn't yell at the Magdalene, so one day the Pope will catch up with the rest of us."

Lulu bubbled over at the mention of the Pope.

"Tommy, tell him about how we saw him when he oamc to Quccns," she gushed. "It was magic. I le walked right past us."

"The Polish Primate," said Tommy, puffing on his cigar, "Sounds like a monkey, doesn't it?" The crackling laughter followed again and then the fit of coughing. Lulu brought him water.

"Isn't it a shame they don't let the old guy marry?" she sighed. "He's got to wank every night, and such a vigorous man for a Pope, not one of those weak old saints in winding sheets."

Tommy protested.

"There's something to be said for staying single," he said, winking at me. "I had someone once and it didn't work out. Didn't do what I said and I was footing the bills. I say if you stay home with an allowance and no bills to pay, you have to keep the house clean and have dinner ready. You got total freedom during the day for whatever, whomever. The only obligations are at night, if you know what I mean. Now I'm a generous guy, Michael, but I don't take no lip and no one says no to me in matters of the heart."

Lulu's eyes widened as she watched for my reaction. A stranger coming into the room would have thought he was abusing me in this sadistic tone rather than telling a story. Everyone knew he was talking about a man but that went unsaid.

"A happy relationship is rare," I vouched. "Better nothing than unhappy."

"Amen," said Lulu, relieved and patting Tommy on the shoulder.

"Billy was a good kid, Tommy," she said.

His face was frozen in an angry grimace.

"We were all virgins when we got married," said the enormous blond daughter in red. "We don't know if our husbands are good or not. How would we know the difference?"

"We are," said Vinnie, patting his belly and belching with a big smile. I could see his erection in his jeans as he sat on the couch.

"We wouldn't know," she repeated, her fat, wide face as innocent as a little girl's.

When it was time to go, Lulu took me aside.

"Did you have a nice time, Michael? Don't you love us? Because we love you, Michael."

"Yes, I love you guys," I assured her, touched.

"Jill came here and sat stiff in the chair and couldn't relax around Tommy and Billy. She told me Tommy gave her the creeps. I say life's too short to think about it. We're all travelers here and we hardly have time to unpack our luggage before we're dead."

I smiled gratefully and told her she was an amazing cook. I thanked her for the doggy bag and she squeezed my cheek.

"Now go out and make us some money."

And then she leaned away from the door, peering around to whisper.

"Don't mind Tommy," she said. "He's into power. When he says shit you say 'what color?' That's just his way. He's very rich as you can tell and maybe you can get him for a client, but he doesn't trust nobody. He's very hush-hush. Doesn't want anyone to know what he's got. He knows what I got but he won't say nothing about himself. We've been feeding him for years and he's getting up there. I hope he remembers us when he dies, because he has no real family besides us now with Billy gone, just the one nephew who works at the parlor, and boy is he cute! You should meet him sometime, Michael. You two might go for each other."

"Let's you and I be lovers," I joked with her. "When Ed goes, call me for the orgy. We'll paint the town red, swap partners, whatever you like."

"Just make me rich, Michael," she laughed. "I don't care what the priest says. If there's a Heaven there's nothing good to do up there. I sure don't want to spend eternity in church. I only want to know if I'm still going to be fat up there, or if I'll finally have the slim body I always dreamed of. Meanwhile, I need more money. No more crappy lies and Limited Partnerships."

A sparrow landed on the bottom stair one foot away from me. Something occurred to me at Athena's prompting.

"Did Jill write anything down?"

"Sure. I have a letter."

"Are you kidding?"

I closed the door again.

"I don't want to get you in trouble, Michael. You think they'll give me something for it? I'll send you the letter."

"Just don't mention that we talked about it."

Lulu filed a complaint against Jill the next week for selling her the 'mutual trust fund', as she called the Limited Partnerships.

"Michael," Gluck demanded when he called me into his office to discuss it. "Did you know anything about this? It's going to cost us."

"I never understood the Limited Partnerships," I said, dodging. "She been rumbling about it since we sold it."

"Michael," said Jill frantically over the phone. "Did you talk to her?"

"I talk to her all the time. I'm her gay son."

"You told her you were gay?" she asked. "Does she know you're sick too?"

"I'm not sick."

The firm gave Lulu twenty thousand dollars, citing Jill's letter promising the original investment was guaranteed.

"Michael, I love you," Lulu sang over the phone.

"Cash the check."

"Don't you want me to invest it in another mutual trust fund?"

"There's no such thing," I said, wary of this Hermes. "How about a six-month CD?"

....

The next major customer to meet was James Hard, an employee at the firm. He had a half million sitting in money market and Jill had warned me that he was unsellable.

"He's religious."

I met him over lunch in the cafeteria of his office because he was anxious about missing work.

He wore a wig that sat on his head like a cat on a perch. He had hair as black as ebony, lips as red as blood, and skin as white as snow. When he shook my hand, his palms were cold and sweaty. He was a walking corpse.

As we sat down to lunch, he took some pamphlets out of his briefcase and laid them on the table.

"Are you a believer?"

I saw Jesus on the cover looking mighty angry at the End of the World and shook my head, 'yes'. I had done my Catechism so I decided to go along for the ride.

"I believe in my Lord, Jesus Christ," I said tentatively. "But I don't like my Church." That part at least was true because of their hostility to gays and women.

"It's good you said that," he answered, looking pleased. "I thought you might have been led astray by the love of money. I've had my doubts about your character in other ways, too. Tell me why you don't like the Church--and I must admit, I'm very pleased to hear you say that, because the Catholic Church is the church of Satan."

I saw my chance to tease the Cyclops.

"I was abused by a priest and I still carry that sin on my soul," I lied, zeroing in on his suspicions. "Do you want to know exactly what he did to me?" I asked, but he shook his head in compassion. I wanted to add the Southern Belle accent but Athena's better judgment stopped me.

"You are deeply troubled."

"I am damaged goods," I admitted. "I've tried to forgive the priest who did it but it's difficult. Do you want to know exactly what he did to me?"

"That's not necessary. Do you pray?"

"I meditate."

His eyes popped out of his lizard face.

"That's Lucifer!" he exclaimed in a panic, and those sitting around us looked up and nodded knowingly at each other. "He is the White Light. You must turn away from him now."

He put his fish hand on my hand as I shook my head in innocence.

"I mean by 'meditate' that I think about Jesus and what he gave to humanity. I like to sit in the chapel—"

"Chapel!" he interrupted, indignant. "You must not worship idols. Are you praying to statues?"

"Lead me out of the darkness," I implored him, groping my way through his maze of thou-shalt-not's.

"Satan is alive and well and living in New York City," he announced, filling me in on the conspiracy. "You need guidance and that one light is Jesus our Lord. So do me a favor, Michael, when you leave here I want you to say 'I believe in Jesus Christ my Savior'. Say it out loud so you can hear it," he said, looking around at the other tables, "but not in here. I've been told not to spread the Word in here anymore."

We had an awkward pause.

"Caesar's rules," he explained as I nodded, mesmerized by his translucent skin like sushi. The bobby pins holding his wig in place stuck out of his hairline.

"You might practice saying it under your breath right now," he told me, anxious to know that my soul would be saved. I presumed he got extra credit for that.

"Jesus Christ is my Savior," I said resolutely, while Hermes watched with a snicker. "I believe in Jesus Christ my Savior."

"Excellent!" he declared, slamming his fork down decisively and standing to offer me an open-armed embrace. I felt a pat on my butt with the slightest hint of grasping but attributed it to chaste awkwardness. To my surprise, we sat down again. I thought lunch was over.

"So are you married, Michael?" he asked me, looking me directly in the eyes.

"No."

"I am for ten years now." This was a surprise coming from the old lizard. "I wandered through life, lonely and unhappy like you, until Kitty came into my life, and I thank Jesus Christ for sending her to me."

I nodded, intrigued by the idea of Jesus as a yenta.

Then his white forehead got stern.

"You must either marry or abhor the flesh," he commanded, "Just let it fall away. Would you rather lose one part of your body or lose the Kingdom of Heaven forever?"

"That's an easy choice," I told him. I had no intention of losing my dick.

He went for the close.

"You have to come to our congregation. We're at Broadway and Fiftieth, right in the heart of Sodom, Sundays at eleven. There are plenty of good Christian souls there to help lead you and strengthen your faith. Maybe you'll find your bride among us."

"I'll come on Sunday."

He gripped my bicep through my suit jacket and squeezed it a couple of times.

"You mustn't try to go it alone," he said, searching my eyes. "It's possible because Jesus says it's possible but it's much harder that way, Michael."

He leaned in closer, still palpating my bicep.

"You are surrounded by temptation. Satan is very near you." He kept pumping my bicep. I shuddered.

"I swear I'll come," I said.

At this he sat up alarmed.

"Don't swear anything. Just say you'll come."

"I'll come," I said, "and it's my birthday Sunday."

Again he ignited.

"Birthdays are pagan holidays. Forget about birthdays."

He relaxed his grip finally and smiled. I realized then that he was wearing lipstick and must be an albino.

"I'll come to Mass," I promised him.

"Service," he corrected me and then chuckled. "Don't sweat it, Michael. You're in good hands."

Again I got up to leave but he opened the pamphlets named 'The Good News' with Fifties style cartoon graphics on the cover. He handed me the one with Jesus throwing lightning bolts at the 'The End of the World'.

"So when is that happening?" I asked breezily.

"No one can know the Lord's intentions," he said solemnly, "but it will be soon. I believe within the next five or six years. There's already war around Kuwait—"

"There's always war over there."

"Kuwait is the former Eden. That's where it starts, but it ends in Armageddon, which is in northern Israel. All we can do is watch the Lord's pattern as it unfolds."

He assumed a look of mystery now and I folded down my lower lip to hide Hermes' sneer. He read the pamphlet over my shoulder while I examined it.

"The artist we hired is excellent," he noted.

"He's got a Muse, that's for sure."

He sat up abruptly.

"Michael, are you mocking me?"

"Certainly not," I insisted, looking serious. "I have a lot to learn, that's all. My heart is true and it longs for the Holy Spirit—"

"Holy Ghost," he stammered.

"I don't expect to understand everything right now," I said, placating, "so I must have patience and seek the Lord at my own pace."

"Amen," he said gratefully, widening his snow-white face into a homey smile with lips sealed as if holding in his dentures. In the back of my mind, Hermes was laughing, but I didn't look in that direction.

It was raining out.

"You'd better get back," he said. "Market hours."

I jumped up.

"Call me this afternoon with bond ideas," he told me. "I've got fifty thousand to invest and I'm looking for ten year maturities."

I couldn't resist.

"What about the world ending in six years?"

"No one knows the mind of the Lord," he said, offering his hand. As I was leaving he added, "And get me the twenty year rate, too."

"See you Sunday."

I hesitated to go to the service but Big Nose assured me I was on a good track.

"They're loaded because they got no vices, those people," he said, "Go bust some Christian bawls."

The congregation was in its Sunday best and heartwarmingly diverse, not the bald and pale missile worshippers of "Planet of the Apes" that I expected. James eagerly introduced me to the members, saying, "this is the stock broker I was talking about" but I noticed they kept peering at me whenever I spoke with anyone. My sincerity was being assessed.

The service lasted over two hours and featured some terrific gospel singing. It was in a massive former movie theater near Times Square. Although the crowd was multi-racial, they all had that lobotomy look of true believers.

One older, slim woman with the bearing of a dancer gravitated towards me.   I considered her my 'fag hag in Christ'.

"How dreadful for you to work amongst the money changers," she said sympathetically.

"They need someone honest down there," I told her, angling.

"The Lord makes no distinctions."

"He seems to like tax men," I noted.

"Former tax men," she corrected me. "He called them away from that evil profession."

"We should abolish the I.R.S.," I blurted out.

"Amen to that!" she said, putting her hand on my shoulder.

"I do what I can to live an upright, godly life," I said, playing forthright. "I don't trade for commissions. I act in the interest of my clients. It's only money, but if I can help a fellow Christian live a comfortable life, I'm ready to be of service. Render unto Caesar--"

I forgot the rest of the quote so I waved my hand and she took it as an abbreviation, so I continued.

"Also, it doesn't hurt to be a believer and set an example for the other brokers in my office. It's funny how they come to me when the going gets tough. When someone dies or is injured, suddenly there's an interest in Jesus and in the Truth."

"God bless you, son," she said, squeezing my shoulder. "You are a most surprising young man." I gave her a hug, as if moved by the moment.

"What do you have for a dividend stock?"

I attended three meetings and opened twelve accounts. When I spoke to these clients, Irony was banished along with all psychological complexity. They were as dense and literal-minded as Herakles the Hero so I cloaked myself in bald sincerity, hiding my sales persona and cultivating the insipid smile of Goodness Incarnate, a dumbed down Christian version of Hestia the Homey with fishhooks pulling up a simple, sealed-lips smile.

"Why dontcha show up in a dress and call yourself the Magdalene?" Big Nose suggested.

Meanwhile James kept buying ten and twenty-year government bonds while lamenting how the country was falling apart.

I tried to be sympathetic.

"It's terrible about the gays and St. Patrick's Day," I said over the phone while Big Nose laughed silently beside me.

"First of all, Patrick was no saint," he told me sternly. "There are too many questions about the snakes. But you're right about that sick life style. They stick it right in our face. They are a symbol of the disintegration of the country."

"Are you patriotic?" I asked him, eager to open another can of worms.

"America was a good country," he said wistfully. "A godly country, but now it's Sodom and Gomorrah all over again. Even Canada is going down the drain. I have relatives in the Argentine and I'm considering retiring there or maybe New Zealand. They haven't ruined that yet."

I remembered a Kiwi who played with me once. He was pretty kinky.

"Do you think Jesus looked like the Caucasian one we see on the crucifix or was he dark like an Israeli?" I asked him.

"He was the son of God."

"Do you think he was handsome? Athletic?" I asked. "You'd think the Son of God would look like a movie star." I didn't mention that you'd think he'd be hung and hot as well.

"That's not relevant, Michael."

"I'm also troubled by the time the Devil came to him to tempt him and after Jesus said, 'no', the angels came to minister to him. What was that about, the ministering to him?" I asked coyly. I always presumed they gave him food, a massage, and a blowjob and maybe did his laundry like Big Nose's girlfriend.

"They were praying with him."

Some comfort after forty days of eating bugs and bitter honey.

. . . .

The other major client I went to see was Dewey Coleman, a sixty-five year old gay man from Oklahoma who inherited a boatload of cash from his lover who died of AIDS.

"Hello, Michael."

He was a Texan and very grand in the way he shook my hand but also a bit fey. Dionysus was hiding in there beneath the ten-gallon hat and the big diamond ring.

"You are not going to sell me any more of those gahdayemed Limited Pahnerships, are you? No Siree. I need to make a small fortune to make up for those lousy investments so I can keep going to my warm places."

"Tangiers, Tunis, Colombo," I said dreamily, "the lands of the gods."

"And you can get anything you want in those godly lands."

"Naughty, naughty," I mock-chided him, matching his camp with my own in Hermes fashion. I took him to dinner and a drag show where a cute Latino boy offered his services in the long multi-cocktail fashion of a hustler who wants to be thought of as a friend who just needs a little help.

I had paid the guy beforehand but Dewey didn't have to know that. He looked a little older than I thought when he went under the light to count the money, but he could still be Dewey's grown son. This was a male version of Aphrodite the Courtesan, the holy priestesses of sexual healing in ancient Corinth, the city of Hermes.

As we were leaving the club, he took me aside to ask me what Dewey was expecting and I told him not to worry.

"He'll probably just want to worship you."

"That's cool, that's cool, way cool," he said, instinctively grasping his crotch.

I handed Dewey a bottle of poppers as he got in the cab with his new lover and wished them well. They were all smiles.

It was true love--at least for a few months--and for once in his life Dewey didn't have to travel to find someone to sleep with. On the phone he sounded like a teenager giddy with love.

"Don't tell me he's 'the One'," I joked.

"Make it the one thousand and first," he answered, so I knew he hadn't gone completely mad with Eros.

Their six months together cost him dearly. They dined out every night and went to the theater and ballet constantly, so I was always sending him checks. Dewey worried that Luis would get bored but the man—whom I would place in his late thirties and towards the end of his hustling years--seemed to genuinely enjoy his company.

At the end of six glorious months, Dewey had a massive coronary in bed after taking a hit of poppers. He died in the embrace of Eros and left the man his money. Suddenly, the one who couldn't spend it fast enough became an apt investor and obsessive saver. He studied tattoo and went to work for a shop in the East Village. No more hustling for him; Dewey had made him respectable. All in all, a good trade, as Hermes would say, considering the circumstances. He kept the account with me and we built a nice portfolio of blue chips.

Closing the Deal

I made the clients my own while paying my dues to Jill every month. I always brought Big Nose with me to meet her and she always brought her girlfriend.

"You got the loot?" she'd ask trying to make a joke of it. We'd share small talk and she would inevitably ask me, "Does Gluck know?" to remind me of the power she held over me.

I was her indentured servant with another eighteen months to go. I felt like I was approaching the Cyclops as my steps grew heavy entering the lovely courtyard on the river with the palm trees arranged under vast skylights.

"She's got nuttin' on ya," said Big Nose. "You should cut her off."

"Gluck can't find out," I repeated.

Standing on the marble floor, I got dizzy as I sensed the power of her approaching spell. Jill appeared out of nowhere, dark and elegant in a purple dress. This time she came alone, looking tall and confident like a goddess.

"Big Nose, are you his familiar?"

"He's my bodyguard," I explained, making light of the truth.

"So is this the hot stuff?" she asked, looking around and taking the paper bag. "Mum's the word. How are you feeling, Michael," sang the Siren.

"See ya," said Big Nose, turning to go, a look of disgust warping his mouth.

"Wait, how are you Michael? I need to know how you feel?" she sang in the concerned, motherly voice she once used on elderly clients.

My suit kept her from seeing the KS all over my body but I still had my muscles.

"Tell me," she said, "What's new with the partnership? Bring me up to date on our clients."

"How do you like your new job?" I volleyed.

"Not much yet," she admitted with a little frown, "How do you feel?"

"Great, Jill, I'm going to live forever."

The late day sun was flooding across the windowed theater, washing the marble floor with an iridescent gold as though bathing the room in wealth. Business people in suits streamed past us on all sides like busy Zeus's and Athena's.

Big Nose pulled my shoulder.

"Nice seein' ya," he repeated.

"Michael," she started in a tone that let me know this was what she was after, "you have a bonus coming for exceeding three hundred thousand in commissions last year. I'm entitled to part of that bonus. That's part of the deal. I should've mentioned it before. You need to give me my share."

"I'll let you know as soon as I know anything about it."

"And there's the Christmas bonus. You'd never have gotten that without me. And the Limited Partnerships give a trailing commission that I'm entitled to, since I've taken all the heat for doing them."

I smiled.

"Gotta go," said Big Nose.

"Kiss-kiss," she said, waving. Then she disappeared into the swarming crowd of commuters.

"In the mob they kiss you before you die," said Big Nose.

I said nothing. Staring her in the face was like staring at Nemesis. Whenever her name appeared on my phone screen I trembled.

My t-cells spurted up on AZT in a month and fell back just as quickly under a hundred, the danger zone where infections lurk like roaming sharks. I was at the mercy of numbers: stock prices, t-cells, months left to pay Jill.

The KS crawled onto my penis and all over my stomach. I had a hundred lesions that were growing progressively darker and thicker. Every two weeks, I went to Dr. Faust who injected them with a noxious drug that made them swell and burst, leaving a weepy scab. Two weeks later when it dried out, it was time for another round, each lesion taking half a dozen visits to treat. Most of them came back after a few months like Lady MacBeth's spots.

"We could leave them," the doctor said sympathetically, "This is largely cosmetic."

"Give me as many shots as you legally can," I instructed him, sprawling naked on the metal table under the fluorescent lights. By the time he finished I was drenched in sweat. We set a limit of 100 shots, including the electric needle that was used on the more sensitive areas. I marveled at the places that could be stuck with a needle—the underarm, the nipple, the head of the penis, the bottoms of the feet—and how hard it is to rise above the pain like Apollo while the needle goes in, especially when there's an electric current.

The needles were the bee stings of Apollo and this was his revenge for my turning my back on him years before. He was the intense focus of raw pain zipping off the end of a needle. The lesions were from Dionysus the Stranger, the Invader living in my body. And the courage to keep going was from Ares, who is *menos,* the second wind that lightens the legs of the weary soldier.

I learned that the gods are not only mental games and metaphors. They are real intrusions into experience. I lay in bed stung in a hundred intimate places oozing and scabbing so we could do it all over again in a ritual to the two gods.

"You're St. Sebastian," Big Nose told me when I showed him my bleeding legs. "You should start showering here at the gym because everybody will support you. Hiding your condition isn't good for you."

"I'm too ashamed."

"You can be ashamed or you can be an inspiration."

I thought about the handsome young man covered in KS I saw changing in the gym years earlier. I never saw him after that one instance and presumed the worst in those terrible years. I remembered how ashamed I'd made him feel by staring with my mouth open. This was the justice of the gods and I had to submit.

At home I put a shot bottle of vodka on the altar in honor of Dionysus. As a gift to the god, I started wearing shorts to the gym and showering with the other guys after years of covering up. It wasn't my decision anymore; let them stare all they want. Some guys did stare and whisper to each other, but one guy came up to me and said, "good for you" and shook my hand, then got out of there before anyone else saw him.

I was anemic and weak but kept the show going on caffeine. When I couldn't stay awake at the office, I would crawl under my desk and take a nap while Rose and Big Nose acted as lookouts.

When Gluck came by, they'd say, "You just missed him," or, "he's getting coffee" or "he went to the bathroom" while I lay resting in the niche under the metal desk.

The amoebic dysentery that followed was more difficult to manage than the KS. I was messing my suit pants constantly. I kept extra underwear in my desk--some days going through four or five pairs—and carried my briefcase with me to the bathroom with plastic bags for storage. I wore suppositories to quell the pain.

My production sagged under the fatigue. One morning when I rolled in at Market open, Gluck angrily led me into his office.

"Look at this list," he said, holding up a print out.

"It shows all the accounts who have done no business in the past year. This is inexcusable," he spewed as I checked over the names.

"What does each of these accounts have in common with the rest?" I asked.

"What?"

"Every one of these accounts is richer this year than last year, so sitting tight was the right thing to do."

His eyes widened with fury.

"You have to start staying nights."

This was too much and Athena intervened with her righteous anger. I pulled up my trousers leg, revealing the swollen, blistering wounds on my calf and ankle. I saw Big Noco and Rosc watching through the plate glass walls.

"I have AIDS," I blurted out, "and I don't want a lawsuit."

There. It was out. I was aghast. So was he, looking at my legs.

He stood quietly and then in a little voice he said, "I see. Just try to keep doing what you're doing." Then he put his hand on my shoulder and said, "Keep at it, champ. We need you to survive."

He shook my hand and I went to my desk in tears and stared at the river. When I turned around he was gone.

"That was great," said Big Nose, slapping me on the back.

"Be careful, I had a couple of shots there."

"So the fucking asshole has a heart after all," said Rose.

"You should go on disability now," Big Nose told me.

I had considered this, but it seemed too irrevocable.

"I don't have savings. What if I'm not approved? What if they give it to me and then take it away?"

"You didn't marry Wall Street," he reminded me. "You came down here on a Hermes stint, as you call it. Maybe it's over."

"We're interested in your accounts," said Rose bluntly, "I'll give you a thousand for each million in assets you sell me. Big Nose wants A to L, I'll take M to Z."

I stared at the river, my Muse. Pepsi was swimming in his goldfish bowl.

The doctor said 'two years' and that was almost a year ago.

It was the end of the month and time to pay Jill again. This time she wore a beige pants suit.

"So you're a WASP now." I said.

"I'm going to dye my hair blond," she laughed. "I went to a party in Greenwich for the new Bond Department head. Beautiful place, lots of money, but everyone kept calling me Maria. It was so strange. I told them over and over *my name is Jill.* By the time I left I was humming, 'I want to live in America, okay by me in America...'"

"For a small fee in America," I sang as I handed her the bag.

She looked into my face but I only let her see me smile.

"I guess bond people are a little vanilla," I said.

"They're bankers," she said drolly. Then she looked me up and down, assessing, but I made a little wave with my hand like the Queen of England and turned around and left.

"She is one psycho," said Big Nose. "She'll tell you she loves you as she eats your body parts."

She called an hour later infuriated. I was expecting her call and put her on speakerphone for Rose and Big Nose to listen in.

"What's the big idea of putting white tulips in the bag?" she demanded. "Where's the money?"

"Gluck knows," I told her, my voice trembling. "There's nothing you can do now."

"You're blackmailing days are over, bitch," said Rose into the speakerphone.

"No one is blackmailing anyone," came the voice trembling through the speaker.

"Swear it by the river," said Big Nose while Rose laughed cruelly, breaking her spell over me.

"Am I on speakerphone?" she asked. "Michael, I never meant to blackmail you."

"Tell a therapist."

I hung up on her.

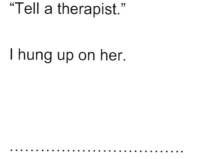

The final break with Wall Street came when a suppository slipped out as I was rushing to the bathroom. It slid down my pants leg and onto the carpet in front of Gluck, who looked at me aghast. Without hesitating or explaining, I bent over and picked up the glistening capsule, wrapping it in a tissue and giving him an ironic smile. I saw one of the secretaries lower her head and pick up the phone. I dreaded what they were saying around the office.

I needed strong magic. I burned some incense at my altar and addressed Hermes with my arms open.

"Hermes," I said, "Show me the way out."

He had given me the gift of friendliness. He had granted me the art of persuasion. He had helped me catch Jill's business, and he had given me AIDS by treating sex as a game. Now I wanted to find the gold purse and vanish the way he did.

I was at the doctor's office perusing a local gay weekly that had an ad for a company called Viatical Settlements, offering to buy life insurance from terminally ill patients. I had sold life insurance as part of my training but was unfamiliar with this idea so I asked Big Nose about it.

"Are you kidding me?" he asked, looking at the ad. "These guys are smart to be in this kind of magazine. You can be a millionaire tomorrow! I bet your doctor will paint a nice picture for them."

My head was reeling. I had come down to Wall Street to make a million dollars. What if the gods grant your wish, but not in the form you imagined? Wouldn't that be just like them?

Sybil asked to live as many years as grains of sand in her hands that she scooped up but she forgot to ask for eternal youth as well. Now she's a cicada in a jar.

What do you want, Sybil, ask the children.

I want to die.

"If you're going to do this," said Big Nose, "You have to do it the right way and look sicker than you are. Let me make a suggestion."

I stopped taking my drugs on Big Nose's advice for a month hoping that my blood tests would worsen.

They did. My doctor was alarmed but I said nothing. I knew I was playing with fire.

His office forwarded the company my medical file and my bloods. All the graphs were pointing to the grave. I felt like Tom Sawyer watching his own funeral as I read the letter about me that my doctor wrote and felt bad for the poor guy, who was Psyche with her mortal tribulations.

Viatical Settlements called with an offer of one million dollars for my life insurance. I stammered my acceptance, faxed the signatures, and the money was in my account three days later.

I took Big Nose and Rose out to dinner to celebrate.

"You have taken a losing situation and turned it to your advantage," said Big Nose with relief.

"What will I do with myself?"

"Go back to your poetry," he roared. "Does Apollo have to hit you over the head? Or do you have a better idea of what to do with whatever time you got left?"

I had often wondered at the strange combination of Hermes and Ares he presented. He was so naturally masculine he reeked of gladiatorial musk, yet his interest in the 'dahk side' kept him low to the ground and sniffing for secrets like the witch goddess. Maybe he was right. Maybe this was what Apollo demanded.

I looked at his face, his big goony face. It was strangely transformed, perhaps by my admiration, perhaps by the excitement, or by the idea of a new life to come. He already seemed a distant memory. I was astonished. He was no longer only Big Nose. He wore the face of a god.

I thought about how Gluck told us to tell ourselves the truth when we put our head on the pillow and there's no one else to bullshit. That's Persephone, the goddess who's married to Hades--to Death himself. Her gorgon faces sees through all pretense.

Rose plopped her hands on the table beside her plate.

"Fuck poetry," she said. "Why don't you write something people will be willing to pay for, Mr. Hermes. Does your precious art have to be only self-expression? Can't it make you a living?"

My mouth gaped.

"I've been listening to you, knucklehead," she said, offended. "Do you think I'm deaf or stupid? Write about the damned gods, since you never shut up about them. People might go for it, because role play is hot."

"Whoa!" chimed in Messero, nodding vigorously and staring at her. "Do that!"

So I was wearing the ruby slippers all along.

It wouldn't matter if no one read what I wrote. My soul would know I was following its call. With the insurance money and the disability, I'd be set for life, however long or short that might be.

I stood in front of my altar burning incense and reciting my thanks to the god while my friends joined in my ceremony of thanksgiving. Each of us put a single white tulip on the altar and said, "Thank you Hermes". A breeze through the window dropped a petal from Rose's flower onto my feet. I picked it up and placed it in front of Peter Pan.

I set up partnerships with Big Nose and Rose—Gluck let me do as I pleased—and spent the next month introducing them to the clients over the phone. God help M to Z, I thought, Rose was going to brutalize them, but my little flock was on its own now and that was Hermes' business, not my own. My t-cells were down to fifty but a new multi-drug therapy was coming to market in the near future that made the doctor optimistic.

"I don't want a going away party," cautioned Gluck, "It would be bad for morale."

Rose and Big Nose walked me to the elevator that last afternoon.

"No phony promises to keep in touch," I told them.

"I'm your broker now," said Big Nose, "and you're one of my best accounts, Mr. Moneybags."

I saw Rose touching his arm.

"Are you two together?" I asked, teasing.

"That's been going on for a year, Dickwad," said Rose.

"I thought you liked disappointed women," I said to Big Nose.

"But I am disappointed," answered Rose, squeezing Big Nose's arm. When he looked in her eyes, his nose in profile, I saw that Eros possessed them completely.

The last elevator ride was like a fall down to Hades, leaving that entire world behind me. As the door opened on the ground floor in front of the dark pool of black granite, I had an uncanny sense that those ten years had gone by in a moment and all those clients and co-workers were already a distant memory. It all seemed to happen to someone else—to some friend of Hermes.

For the first month, I slept day and night, smoking pot and racking up points for St. Peter, who was going to be pleased.

....

I flew to Athens and took the ferry over to Mykonos, where I took a room in a guesthouse on the Aegean a few miles above the busy harbor and the discos where I danced every weekend. Three times I went to Delos to wander over the ruins of Apollo's temple in the heat of the afternoon.

One warm August I was sitting at the bar when a familiar-sounding voice yelled, "Banana!" from across the room.

"What the fuck are you doing here?"

"I live here now, Banana," said Jim, all smiles.

We went back to his palatial home with a pool and gardens a couple of miles from the town, full of news and nostalgia.

"I made a killing," he said. I was thrilled for him. Hermes doesn't envy success—he just wants to enjoy it.

I moved in for the rest of the summer. We lay naked by the pool looking at the many art books in his white stucco library and honored Eros in the usual ways. As I held his penis in my hand, he declaimed, "These are the wrinkles that never grow old."

This was a Hermes affair and all about pleasure. No future was implicated. Hera the Spouse was completely absent. At the end of summer I would be ready to return to the homey self of Hestia back in Chelsea with Dusty climbing on the counter, a part of life that was its own little statue.

The last day on the island Jim went into town shopping. I had seen banana bread on his list so I knew there was some sort of pun in the making.

I put on my bathing suit and walked across the empty courtyard to the stony edge of the water, where the nasturtiums clung to the ledge and the water was crystal clear. I stood on the rock farthest out and held out my arms out in greeting.

"Hermes," I said, "Thank you from the bottom of my heart. Now I'm going to pay attention to other gods for a while."

I jumped in the water and swam out over my head keeping my back to the shore. I imagined the salt water washing Wall Street Hermes away—but not completely away. No god can be eliminated, but he can become like a friend you call on the phone once in a while instead of living together. The bathhouse and booth stores would remain Hermes' sacred temples, but I was done with sales.

I stayed in the water until even the warm Aegean gave me goose bumps, and when I had enough and had washed the salt away, I pulled on some white shorts and a dolphin t-shirt and I sat on the white chaise in the courtyard watching the uncannily blue water scintillate in the brightness of day.

I plucked a lemon for my Campari from a branch overhanging my chair and cut wedges with a small knife.

Other gods wanted other things from me now so I started jotting down notes on a blue pad.

Perhaps a book would honor both Hermes and Apollo at the same time—a how-to book that shows how to befriend any god, provided that god is open to friendship with you. After all, if you want to be someone else, *you* don't have to change. You only have to befriend some other person in the psyche who was there all along, like the ruby slippers. The way to be someone else is to let someone else be *me.*

And so, Friend, I wander off like an alluring stranger you followed down a dark street, who once seemed too charming to betray you and too friendly to rob you blind and turned out to be the Thief of the Night.

Made in the USA
Middletown, DE
22 May 2020